The Observers Series
AIRCRAFT

About the Book

Observers Aircraft is the indispensable pocket guide to the world's latest aeroplanes, helicopters and tilt-rotor aircraft, and the most recent versions of established types. This, the thirty-ninth edition, embraces the latest civil and military aeroplanes and rotorcraft of twenty countries. Its scope ranges from such airliner newcomers as the Airbus A340, the BAe Jetstream 41, the Canadair RJ and the Deutsche Aerospace (Do) 328, through general aviation débutantes, such as the BAe 1000, the Pilatus PC-12 and the Swearingen-Jaffe SJ 30, to a variety of new military aircraft that include the McDonnell Douglas C-17A heavy lift freighter, the Chinese NAMC K-8 basic trainer and light attack aircraft, and the configurationally innovative YF-22 and YF-23, competing, as this edition closed for press, to fulfil the USAF's Advanced Tactical Fighter requirement. All data has been checked and revised as necessary, and more than seventy-five per cent of the three-view silhouettes are new or have been revised for this edition.

About the Author

William Green, compiler of *Observers Aircraft* for forty years, is internationally known for many works of aviation reference. He entered aviation journalism during the early years of World War II, subsequently serving with the Royal Air Force and resuming aviation writing in 1947. Until recently, William Green was managing editor of the monthly *AIR International*, one of the largest-circulation European-based aviation journals, and co-editor of its thrice-annual companion publication, *AIR Enthusiast*.

The *Observer's* series was launched in 1937 with the publication of *The Observer's Book of Birds*. Today, over fifty years later, paperback *Observers* continue to offer practical, useful information on a wide range of subjects, and with every book regularly revised by experts, the facts are right up-to-date. Students, amateur enthusiasts and professional organisations alike will find the latest *Observers* invaluable.

'Thick and glossy, briskly informative' – *The Guardian*

'If you are a serious spotter of any of the things the series deals with the books must be indispensable' – *The Times Educational Supplement*

O B S E R V E R S

AIRCRAFT

William Green

With silhouettes by Dennis Punnett

FREDERICK WARNE

AIRBUS A310-300

Country of Origin: International consortium.
Type: Short- to medium-haul commercial transport.
Power Plant: Two 53,500 lb st (238 kN) General Electric CF6-80A3 or 59,000 lb st (262·4 kN) CF6-80C2A8 turbofans, or 52,000 lb st (231·2 kN) Pratt & Whitney PW4152 or 56,000 lb st (249·1 kN) PW4156A turbofans.
Performance: Max cruise speed, 557 mph (897 km/h) at 35,000 ft (10 670 m); long-range cruise, 528 mph (850 km/h) at 37,000 ft (11 280 m); range with 218 passengers and international reserves (CF6-80C2A2 engines), 5,090 mls (8 191 km), (PW4152 engines), 5,160 mls (8 300 km).
Weights: Operational empty, 175,907–176,017 lb (79 790–79 840 kg); max take-off, 330,695 lb (150 000 kg).
Accommodation: Flight crew of two (with provision for third and fourth crew seats) and maximum capacity for up to 280 passangers nine abreast. Typical two-class layout for 18 first-class passengers six abreast and 200 economy-class passengers eight abreast.
Status: Prototype flown 3 April 1982, and first deliveries (Lufthansa and Swissair) commencing 29 March 1983. Extended range -300 version first flown 8 July 1985, with deliveries commencing (to Swissair) on following 17 December. Total of 215 A310s (all versions) ordered by beginning of 1991 with 178 delivered and when production (together with that of the A300 which see) was continuing at four aircraft monthly.
Notes: By comparison with the A300, the A310 has a new wing of reduced size and a shorter fuselage. The -300 version was the first production airliner with an additional fuel tank in the tailplane and the first to employ carbonfibre-reinforced plastic for a major structural element (the fin).

AIRBUS A310-300

Dimensions: Span, 144 ft 0 in (43,90 m); length, 153 ft 1 in (46,66 m); height, 51 ft 10 in (15,81 m); wing area, 2,357·3 sq ft (219,00 m²).

AIRBUS A340

Country of Origin: International consortium.

Type: Long-haul commercial transport.

Power Plant: Four 31,200 lb st (138·8 kN) CFM International CFM56-5C2 turbofans.

Performance: (Estimated -200) Max cruise speed, 568 mph (914 km/h) at 37,000 ft (11 300 m); econ cruise, 541 mph (871 km/h) at 40,000 ft (12 200 m); max operating altitude, 41,000 ft (12 500 m); range (with 262 passengers), 8,700 mls (14 000 km), (max fuel and 57,900-lb/26 250-kg payload), 9,196 mls (14 800 km).

Weights: (-200) Operational empty, 269,200 lb (122 100 kg); max take-off, 558,900 lb (253 500 kg).

Accommodation: Flight crew of two and (-200) typical three-class arrangement for 18 first, 78 business and 170 economy class passengers in seven-, eight and nine-abreast seating, all with twin aisles. Maximum of 375 passengers nine abreast.

Status: Launched on 5 June 1987 (in parallel with the A330), the A340 is being offered in -200 and -300 versions, and the latter is scheduled to be the first to fly, this event being anticipated in October 1991. Both versions are expected to enter commercial service late 1992, and firm orders had been placed for 89 by the beginning of 1991.

Notes: The A340 is being developed in parallel with the twin-engined A330, which, scheduled to enter flight test in the autumn of 1992, has wing, cockpit and tail commonality, and the same basic fuselage. The two aircraft will differ essentially in the number of engines and in engine-related systems. The A340-200 (described and illustrated above) is a very-long-range version of the basic design, the A340-300 trading range for passenger capacity, its fuselage being lengthened (opposite page) to provide projected maximum accommodation for 440 passengers. The A340-300 Combi will typically carry six freight pallets and 194 passengers in a three-class layout.

AIRBUS A340-300

Dimensions: Span, 197 ft 10 in (60,30 m); length, 206 ft 3¾ in (62,88 m); height, 55 ft 2 in (16,83 m); wing area, 3,908·4 sq ft (363,10 m²).

AIRTECH (CASA/IPTN) CN-235-100

Countries of Origin: Spain and Indonesia.
Type: Regional commercial transport and (CN-235M) military freighter.
Power Plant: Two 1,750 hp (1,305 kW) General Electric CT7-9C turboprops.
Performance: Max cruise speed, 281 mph (452 km/h) at 15,000 ft (4 575 m); max initial climb, 1,525 ft/min (7,75 m/sec); service ceiling, 26,600 ft (8 110 m); range (with reserves at 18,000 ft/5 485 m and range cruise), 770 mls (1 240 km) with max payload, 2,429 mls (3 910 km) with max fuel.
Weights: Operational empty, 20,725 lb (9 400 kg); max take-off, 33,290 lb (15 100 kg).
Accommodation: Flight crew of two with basic arrangement for 45 passengers in four-abreast seating with central aisle. The CN-235-QC (Quick Change) version offers various combinations of passengers and standard LD2 or LD3 containers (eg, 19 passengers and two LD3 containers).
Status: First prototype flown (in Spain) on 11 November 1983 and second (in Indonesia) on 31 December 1983. First customer delivery (Merpati Nusantara) 15 December 1986. By the beginning of 1991, 53 had been ordered for airline service and 62 by military customers (Botswana, Ecuador, France, Indonesia and Saudi Arabia), and a preliminary agreement had been reached for assembly and progressive manufacture of 52 under licence in Turkey.
Notes: The CN-235 is manufactured jointly by CASA in Spain and IPTN in Indonesia (through the jointly-owned Aircraft Technology Industries, or Airtech) on a 50-50 basis without component duplication. Initial production aircraft with CT7-7A engines were designated Series 10, and from the 31st aircraft CT7-9C engines and new nacelles resulted in the Series 100.

AIRTECH (CASA/IPTN) CN-235-100

Dimensions: Span, 84 ft 7¾ in (25,81 m); length, 70 ft 0½ in (21,35 m); height, 26 ft 10 in (8,18 m); wing area, 636·17 sq ft (59,10 m²).

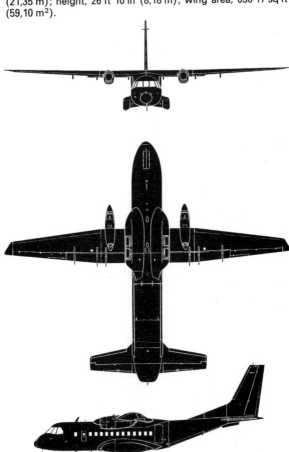

AMX INTERNATIONAL AMX

Countries of Origin: Italy and Brazil.

Type: Single-seat battlefield support and two-seat (AMX-T) operational trainer and maritime attack aircraft.

Power Plant: One 11,030 lb st (49·1 kN) Rolls-Royce Spey Mk 807 turbofan.

Performance (AMX): Max speed (at 23,700 lb/10 750 kg), 568 mph (913 km/h) at 36,000 ft (10 975 m), or Mach=0·86; max initial climb, 10,250 ft/min (52 m/sec) at 28,660 lb/13 000 kg), 328 mls (528 km) LO-LO-LO with 5 min combat and 10 per cent reserves, HI-LO-HI, 576 mls (926 km); ferry range (max external fuel and 10 per cent reserves), 2,073 mls (3 336 km).

Weights: Operational empty, 14,638 lb (6 640 kg); max take-off, 28,660 lb (13 000 kg).

Armament: One 20-mm rotary cannon (Italian) or two 30-mm cannon (Brazilian), two AIM-9L Sidewinder or similar self-defence AAMs. External ordnance load of 8,377 lb (3 800 kg).

Status: First of seven AMX prototypes flown (in Italy) 15 May 1984, two of these being assembled in Brazil with first flying on 16 October 1986. The first Italian series aircraft flown on 11 May 1988, and first Brazilian on 12 August 1989. First and second Italian AMX-T two-seaters flown 14 March and 16 July 1990. Current planning calls for 187 single-seaters and 51 two-seaters for the Italian Air Force and 79 aircraft including 15 two-seaters for the Brazilian Air Force. Nearly 50 AMX aircraft (including three AMX-Ts) produced by beginning of 1991.

Notes: The AMX is being built by Alenia (46·7%) and Aermacchi (23·6%) in Italy and Embraer (29·7%) in Brazil, with three assembly lines and no component manufacturing duplication. The two-seat AMX-T (illustrated) is being developed for maritime attack and other combat roles.

Dimensions: Span (over missiles), 32 ft 8½ in (9,97 m); length, 43 ft 5⅜ in (13,23 m); height, 14 ft 11⅛ in (4,55 m); wing area, 226·04 sq ft (21,00 m²).

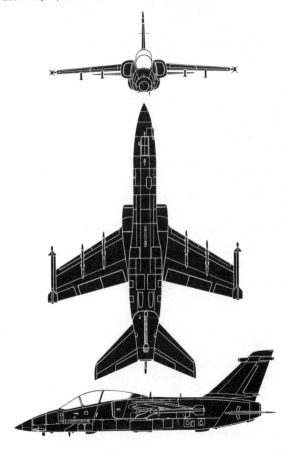

ANTONOV AN-72 (COALER)

Country of Origin: USSR.

Type: Light civil and military STOL transport.

Power Plant: Two 14,330 lb st (63·74 kN) ZMKB (Lotarev) D-36 or 16,534 lb st (73·6 kN) D-436K turbofans.

Performance: (D-36 turbofans) Max speed, 438 mph (705 km/h); normal cruise, 342 mph (550 km/h) at 26,250–32,800 ft (8 000–10 000 m); range (with 22,045-lb/10 000-kg payload), 715 mls (1 150 km), (with 3,307-lb/1 500-kg payload), 2,610 mls (4 200 km); service ceiling, 32,810 ft (10 000 m).

Weights: Max take-off (from 3,280-ft/1 000-m runway), 60,625 lb (27 500 kg), or (from 5,905-ft/1 800-m runway), 76,060 lb (34 500 kg).

Accommodation: Pilot and co-pilot/navigator on flight deck, plus provison for flight engineer, and sidewall folding seats and removable central seats for 68 passengers, or 57 paratroops, or (medevac) 24 casualty stretchers with provison for 12 seated casualties and a medical attendant.

Status: First of two An-72 prototypes (Coaler-A) flown on 22 December 1977, with extensively revised pre-series (eight) An-72 (Coaler-C) following in 1985. This pre-series included two of the An-74 (Coaler-B) version for operation in the Arctic and Antarctic. Series production commenced at Kharkov facility in 1987, and was continuing at a rate of 20 annually (all versions) at the beginning of 1991.

Notes: The An-72 makes use of the 'Coanda effect' to achieve STOL performance, engine exhaust gases flowing over the wing upper surfaces and inboard slotted flaps. The An-74 version (illustrated above) has a flight crew of five, advanced navaids and provision for a wheel/ski undercarriage.

ANTONOV AN-72 (COALER)

Dimensions: Span, 104 ft 7½ in (31,89 m); length, 92 ft 1¼ in (26,07 m); height, 28 ft 4½ in (8,65 m); wing area, 1,061·57 sq ft (98,62 m²).

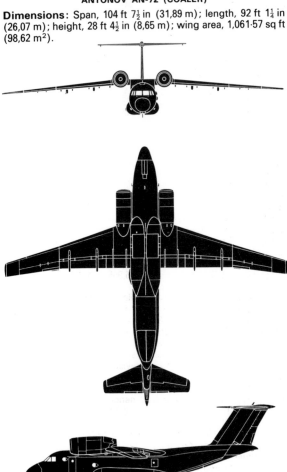

ANTONOV AN-124 RUSLAN (CONDOR)

Country of origin: USSR.

Type: Long-range heavy-lift freight transport.

Power plant: Four 51,590 lb st (229·5 kN) ZMKB (Lotarev) D-18T turbofans.

Performance: Max cruise speed, 537 mph (865 km/h); normal cruise, 497–528 mph (800–850 km/h) at 32,810–39,370 ft (10 000–12 000 m); range with 330,693-lb/150 000-kg payload, 2,795 mls (4 500 km), (with max fuel), 10,250 mls (16 500 km).

Weights: Max take-off, 892,857 lb (405 000 kg).

Accommodation: Flight crew of six and upper deck seating for relief crews and up to 88 personnel. Lower deck can accommodate all elements of the RSD-10 (SS-20 *Saber*) mobile intermediate-range ballistic missile system, and the largest Soviet tanks and armoured personnel carriers.

Status: First of three prototypes was flown on 26 December 1982, series production being initiated during 1984, with 20 completed by 1989, since which time production has continued at a rate of 10 per annum. Some 40 had been delivered by the beginning of 1991, approximately half of these having been supplied (since 1987) to VTA heavy-lift military units.

Notes: The An-124 is named Ruslan after a character in Russian folklore, and, until the appearance of the derivative An-225, was the world's largest and heaviest aircraft. The An-124 is progressively replacing the An-22 in service with the Soviet Air Force, and the Indian Air Force is expected to receive an initial batch of three transports of this type in 1991–92. The An-124 is designed for simultaneous nose and tail loading, with a visor-type lifting nose and integral forward-folding ramp. It can operate from unprepared fields, hard-packed snow and ice-covered swamp.

ANTONOV AN-124 RUSLAN (CONDOR)

Dimensions: Span, 240 ft 5¾ in (73,30 m); length, 228 ft 0¼ in (69,50 m); height, 73 ft 9¾ in (22,50 m); wing area, 6,760 sq ft (628 m²).

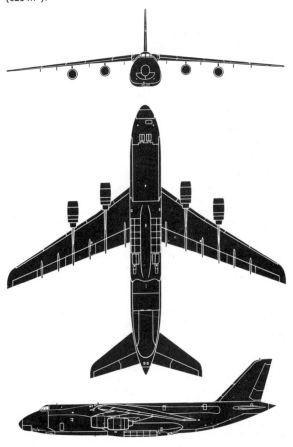

ANTONOV AN-225 MRIYA (COSSACK)

Country of Origin: USSR.

Type: Ultra heavy transport.

Power plant: Six 51,590 lb st (229·5 kN) ZMKB (Lotarev) D-18T turbofans.

Performance: Max cruise speed, 528 mph (850 km/h); normal cruise (internal payload), 435–466 mph (700–750 km/h); range (with 440,917-lb/200 000-kg payload), 2,796 mls (4 500 km).

Weights: Max take-off, 1,322,750 lb (600 000 kg).

Accommodation: Basic flight crew of six (pilot, co-pilot, navigator, communications specialist and two flight engineers) with provision for loadmaster. Rest area for relief crew and cabin for 60–70 personnel above freight hold which is 141 ft (43 m) in length. A load of up to 551,145 lb (250 000 kg) may be carried internally or externally. External loads include a Buran space orbiter, elements of its Energiya rocket launch vehicle or large missile systems which are carried above the fuselage.

Status: First prototype An-225 was flown on 21 December 1988, and a second has since been funded for the support of Soviet space programmes.

Notes: The An-225 Mriya (Dream) has been developed from the An-124 Ruslan and is by far the world's largest and heaviest aircraft, being the first to fly with a gross weight exceeding one million pounds. Primarily intended to participate in the Soviet space programme with outsize loads carried on top of the fuselage, the An-225 can perform more conventional transportation tasks. On 22 March 1989, the prototype established no fewer than 106 world and class records during a three-and-a-half hour flight from Kiev.

ANTONOV AN-225 MRIYA (COSSACK)

Dimensions: Span, 290 ft 0 in (88,40 m); length, 275 ft 7 in (984,00 m); height, 59 ft 4½ in (18,10 m).

ATR (AEROSPATIALE/ALENIA) 72

Countries of Origin: France and Italy.

Type: Regional commercial transport.

Power plant: Two 2,160 shp (1,611 kW) Pratt & Whitney Canada PW124/2 turboprops.

Performance: Max cruise speed, 329 mph (530 km/h) at 25,000 ft (7 620 m); econ cruise, 286 mph (460 km/h) at 25,000 ft (7 620 m); range (at 47,400 lb/21 500 kg), 742 mls (1 195 km) with 16,535-lb (7 500-kg) payload, 1,657 mls (2 666 km) with 66 passengers, 2,727 mls (4 389 km) with zero payload.

Weights: Operational empty, 26,896 lb (12 200 kg); max take-off, 44,070 lb (19 990 kg), (optional), 47,400 lb (21 500 kg).

Accommodation: Flight crew of two and optional arrangements for 64, 66 or 70 passengers, or a high-density arrangement for 74 passengers. Four abreast seating with central aisle.

Status: Prototype ATR 72 flew 27 October 1988, with second and third aircraft following on 20 December 1988 and in April 1989 respectively. Customer deliveries (to KarAir) initiated 27 October 1989. Total of 206 on order and option by 1991 when production rate (combined ATR 42 and 72) was six monthly and to rise to eight monthly by 1994.

Notes: A stretched derivative of the ATR 42 (for which orders and options totalled 332 by the beginning of 1991), the ATR 72 is 14 ft 9 in (4,50 m) longer than the 42–50 passenger aircraft, and is the first commercial airliner with a carbon-fibre wing box, composites forming 30 per cent of the wing structure. The ATR 42 and ATR 72 are manufactured on a 50–50 basis by Aérospatiale of France and Alenia (formerly Aeritalia) of Italy with a joint management company Avions de Transport Régional (ATR). The ATR 72 has an optional higher gross weight (as indicated above), and the ATR 72-210, launched in 1990, is intended for 'hot and high' operation with uprated PW127 engines. Maritime patrol versions of both the ATR 42 and 72 are currently on offer as the Petrel 42 and 72 respectively, and freight-carrying and military versions are available.

ATR (AEROSPATIALE/ALENIA) 72

Dimensions: Span, 88 ft 9 in (27,05 m); length, 89 ft $1\frac{1}{2}$ in (27,17 m); height, 25 ft $1\frac{1}{4}$ in (7,65 m); wing area, 656·6 sq ft (61,00 m²).

BEECHCRAFT SUPER KING AIR 350

Country of Origin: USA.

Type: Light corporate executive or regional transport.

Power Plant: Two 1,050 shp (783 kW) Pratt & Whitney Canada PT6A-60A turboprops.

Performance: Max speed, 362 mph (582 km/h); max cruise (at 12,000 lb/5 443 kg), 360 mph (580 km/h) at 24,000 ft (7 315 m); range cruise, 273 mph (439 km/h) at 35,000 ft (10 670 m); max initial climb (at 14,000 lb/6 350 kg), 2,979 ft/min (15,13 m/sec); max range (45 min reserves), 2,263 mls (3 641 km) at 35,000 ft (10 670 m), 1,639 mls (2 639 km) at 18,000 ft (5 485 m).

Weights: Empty, 9,051 lb (4 105 kg); max take-off, 15,000 lb (6 804 kg).

Accommodation: Pilot and co-pilot/passenger on flight deck and standard arrangement in main cabin for eight passengers in double club seating.

Status: The Super King Air 350 was first flown in September 1988, customer deliveries commencing on 6 March 1990.

Notes: A successor to the Super King Air 300, the 350 embodies a 2 ft 10 in (0,86 m) fuselage stretch, a 1 ft 6 in (0,46 m) increase in wing span, 2 ft (0,61 m) high winglets and two additional windows. More than 4,000 King Airs and Super King Airs have been delivered since introduction of the former in 1964, some 10 per cent of these being supplied to the US Armed Forces for a variety of missions.

BEECHCRAFT SUPER KING AIR 350

Dimensions: Span, 57 ft 11 in (17,65 m); length, 46 ft 8 in (14,22 m); height, 14 ft 4 in (4,37 m); wing area, 310 sq ft (28,80 m²).

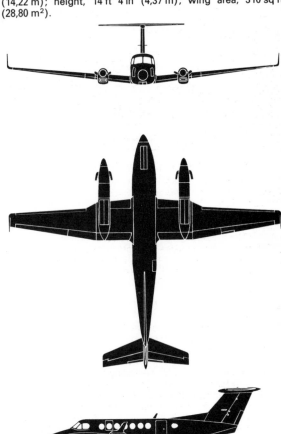

BEECHCRAFT MODEL 1900D

Country of Origin: USA.

Type: Short-haul regional transport.

Power Plant: Two 1,280 shp (955 kW) Pratt & Whitney Canada PT6A-67D turboprops.

Performance: Max cruise speed (at 15,500 lb/7 030 kg), 312 mph (502 km/h) at 10,000 ft (3 050 m), 335 mph (539 km/h) at 20,000 ft (6 095 m); max initial climb (at 16,950 lb/7 688 kg), 2,320 ft/min (11,78 m/sec); service ceiling, 25,000 ft (7 620 m); range (with 19 passengers and IFR reserves), 518 mls (834 km) at 8,000 ft (2 440 m), 587 mls (945 km) at 16,000 ft (4 875 m), 708 mls (1 140 km) at 25,000 ft (7 620 m).

Weights: Operational empty, 10,360 lb (4 699 kg); max take-off, 16,950 lb (7 688 kg).

Accommodation: Flight crew of one or two on flight deck and standard cabin arrangement for 19 passengers in single seats on each side of central aisle and three seats against rear bulkhead.

Status: The prototype Model 1900D first flew on 1 March 1990, certification being anticipated early 1991, with initial deliveries (to Mesa Airlines) mid-1991.

Notes: The Model 1900D is a development of the Model 1900C (of which some 200 had been delivered by the beginning of 1991) featuring a deeper fuselage with 28·5 per cent more volume, a flat floor offering stand-up headroom, and larger cabin windows and door. The Model 1900D also features an enlarged aft cargo door, the cargo hold offering 175 cu ft (4,95 m³) of pressurised space.

BEECHCRAFT MODEL 1900D

Dimensions: Span, 57 ft 10¾ in (17,65 m); length, 57 ft 10⅞ in (17,60 m); height, 14 ft 10⅝ in (4,60 m); wing area, 303 sq ft (28,15 m²).

BEECHCRAFT MODEL 2000 STARSHIP 1

Country of Origin: USA.

Type: Light corporate executive transport.

Power Plant: Two 1,200 shp (895 kW) Pratt & Whitney Canada PT6A-67A turboprops.

Performance: Max cruise speed, 387 mph (622 km/h) at 25,000 ft (7 620 m), 350 mph (563 km/h) at 35,000 ft (10 670 m); econ cruise, 340 mph (546 km/h) at 35,000 ft (10 670 m); max initial climb, 3,225 ft/min (16,38 m/sec); range (at max range power), 1,946 mls (3 132 km) at 35,000 ft (10 670 m).

Weights: Empty equipped, 9,887 lb (4 484 kg); max take-off, 14,400 lb (6 531 kg).

Accommodation: Provision for two crew members on flight deck and standard seating for eight passengers, six in double club arrangement and two on couch.

Status: First of three prototypes flown on 15 February 1986, FAA certification being obtained on 14 June 1988, and first production aircraft flown on 25 April 1989. Ten Starships delivered during 1990, and production tempo of one per month at beginning of 1991 rising to two aircraft monthly.

Notes: The Starship, in mating an aft-mounted laminar-flow wing with a variable-sweep foreplane, is highly innovative in concept. Foreplane sweep changes automatically with flap extension to provide pitch-trim compensation. The first pressurised all-composite aircraft to be certified, the Starship uses such materials as boron, carbon, Kevlar and glassfibre. The canard arrangement renders stalling impossible in landing and take-off.

Dimensions: Span, 54 ft 0 in (16,46 m); length, 46 ft 1 in (14,05 m); height, 12 ft 10 in (3,91 m); wing area, 280·9 sq ft (26,09 m²).

BELL/BOEING V-22 OSPREY

Country of Origin: USA.
Type: Multi-mission tilt-rotor aircraft.
Power Plant: Two 6,150 shp (4,586 kW) Allison T406-AD-400 turboshafts.
Performance: (Manufacturer's estimates) Max cruise speed (aeroplane mode), 316 mph (509 km/h) at sea level, 345 mph (556 km/h) at optimum altitude, (helicopter mode), 115 mph (185 km/h) at sea level; max forward speed with max slung load (15,000 lb/6 804 kg), 230 mph (370 km/h); range (vertical take-off with 12,000-lb/5 443-kg payload), 1,382 mls (2 224 km), (short take-off with 20,000-lb/9 072-kg payload), 2,073 mls (3 336 km); ferry range, 2,418 mls (3 892 km).
Weights: Empty equipped, 31,886 lb (14 463 kg); normal loaded (VTO), 47,500 lb (21 545 kg), (STO) 55,000 lb (29 947 kg); max short take-off, 60,500 lb (27 442 kg).
Accommodation: Normal flight crew of three and up to 24 combat-equipped troops, 12 casualty stretchers plus attendants, or an equivalent cargo load.
Status: First of six flying prototypes entered flight test on 9 March 1989, and the fifth was scheduled to fly in February 1991. A decision concerning series production is expected to be taken late 1991.
Notes: Developed jointly by Bell and Boeing, the Osprey was intended to meet the US Defense Department's Joint Services Advanced Vertical Lift Aircraft requirement. Proposed funding for initial production was deleted from the US Fiscal 1990 and 1991 defense budgets, and the future of the programme remained uncertain at the beginning of 1991.

BELL/BOEING V-22 OSPREY

Dimensions: Span (over rotors), 84 ft 8½ in (25,77 m); 'ength, 62 ft 7⅔ in (19,09 m); height (over tail), 17 ft 7¾ in (5,38 m).

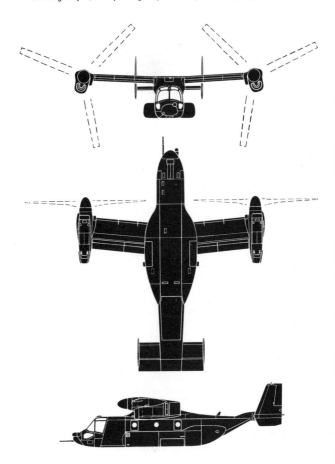

BERIEV A-40 ALBATROSS

Country of Origin: USSR.
Type: Multi-role amphibian.
Power Plant: Two 26,500 lb st (117·7 kN) Perm MKB (Soloviev) D-30KPV turbofans.
Performance: No details had been made available at the time of closing for press.
Weights: Normal loaded weight, 140,000–150,000 lb (63 505–68 040 kg).
Accommodation: (ASR mission) Flight crew of four plus rescue team (with power boats, liferafts and other specialised equipment) and provision for up to 60 survivors.
Status: First of two prototypes of the A-40 reportedly flown during 1988, with second joining the test programme in 1989. No production believed to have commenced by the beginning of 1991.
Notes: Currently the world's only jet-powered amphibian, the A-40 Albatross is, according to Soviet sources, intended specifically for the search-and-rescue mission, but it is believed to have been designed as a multi-role aircraft with a possible ASW/surveillance/minelaying task. The A-40 established a number of international records in its class in September 1989, the most significant of these being a sustained altitude of 43,572 ft (13 281 m) with a load of 22,046 lb (10 000 kg) after taking-off at 152,560 lb (69 200 kg). A 20-ft (6,10-m) stores bay is included in the bottom of the hull, the mainwheel bogies are accommodated by the large pods under the wing roots, the fuselage-side hatches are provided with mechanical ramps and there is provision for in-flight refuelling.

BERIEV A-40 ALBATROSS

Dimensions: Span, 137 ft 1½ in (41,80 m); length (excluding nose probe), 141 ft 0 in (43,00 m).

BOEING 737-500

Country of Origin: USA.

Type: Short- to medium-haul commercial transport.

Power Plant: Two 20,000 lb st (88·97 kN) or (derated) 18,500 lb st (82·29 kN) CFM International CFM56-3B-1 turbofans.

Performance: (Derated engines) Max cruise speed (at 110,000 lb/49 900 kg), 567 mph (912 km/h) at 26,000 ft (7 925 m), range cruise, 494 mph (795 km/h) at 35,000 ft (10 670 m); range (max payload), 1,565 mls (2 519 km) at 482 mph (776 km/h) at 35,000 ft (10 670 m), (with max fuel), 3,970 mls (6 389 km).

Weights: Operational empty, 68,260 lb (30 963 kg); max take-off, 115,500 lb (52 390 kg), (optional), 133,500 lb (60 554 kg).

Accommodation: Flight crew of two and up to 132 passengers six abreast with single aisle, or typical mixed-class arrangement for 108 passengers.

Status: The first 737-500 was flown on 30 June 1989, with first customer delivery (to Southwest) on 28 February 1990. Orders and options for some 220 737-500s by beginning of 1991 from total of 1,741 second-generation (ie, -300, -400 and -500) 737s, these having been preceded by 1,144 first-generation (ie, pre -300) aircraft. The 2,000th delivered on 25 February 1991.

Notes: The smallest of the CFM56-powered 'second-generation' Boeing 737s which share recontoured wing leading edges, extended wings and tailplanes, and more advanced technology, the -500 replaced the 'first-generation' -200. When equipped with auxiliary fuel tanks and the higher-rated engines, the high gross weight -500 has a maximum range of 3,450 miles (5 552 km) with 108 passengers in mixed class accommodation. The Boeing 737 is the world's best-selling commercial airliner and has been in continuous production in progressively improved versions for 24 years.

BOEING 737-500

Dimensions: Span, 94 ft 9 in (28,90 m); length, 101 ft 9 in (31,01 m); height, 36 ft 6 in (11,12 m); wing area, 980 sq ft (91,04 m²).

BOEING 747-400

Country of Origin: USA.

Type: Long-haul commercial transport.

Power Plant: (Options) Four 57,900 lb st (257·5 kN) General Electric CF6-80C2B4, 56,750 lb st (252·39 kN) Pratt & Whitney PW4256, or 58,000 lb st (258 kN) Rolls-Royce RB211-524G turbofans.

Performance: (RB211) Max speed, 606 mph (976 km/h) at 30,000 ft (9 150 m); max cruise, 583 mph (939 km/h) at 35,000 ft (10 670 m); range cruise, 564 mph (907 km/h); range (412 passengers and typical reserves), 8,406 mls (13 528 km).

Weights: (RB211) Operational empty, 393,880 lb (178 661 kg); max take-off (options), 800,000 lb (362 875 kg), 850,000 lb (385 555 kg), or 870,000 lb (394 625 kg).

Accommodation: Flight crew of two and typical three-class seating for 450 passengers with maximum of 660 passengers.

Status: First 747-400 flown on 29 April 1988, with customer deliveries (to Northwest Orient) commencing on 26 January 1989. Three hundred and ninety-four -400s on firm order by beginning of 1991, these following 248 -100s, 393 -200s and 81 -300s.

Notes: The current production version of the Boeing 747, the -400, differs in a number of respects from the preceding -300 which incorporated structural changes to the upper deck area increasing upper deck accommodation to 69 (economy class) passengers. The most significant external changes of the -400 are an extended wing and vertical winglets. Extensive changes have been introduced in most systems, the engine nacelles have been retailored and their struts redesigned. A Combi cargo/passenger version is designated 747-400M and an all-cargo version is designated 747-400F.

BOEING 747-400

Dimensions: Span, 211 ft 0 in (64,31 m); length, 231 ft 10¼ in (70,67 m); height, 63 ft 4 in (19,30 m); wing area, 5,650 sq ft (524,88 m²).

BOEING 757-200

Country of origin: USA.

Type: Short- to medium-haul commercial transport.

Power Plant: (Options) Two 37,400 lb st (166·4 kN) Rolls-Royce RB211-535C or 40,100 lb st (178·4 kN) -535E4, 38,200 lb st (170 kN) Pratt & Whitney PW2037 or 41,700 lb st (185·5 kN) PW2040 turbofans.

Performance: (RB211-535E4) Max cruise speed, 570 mph (917 km/h) at 30,000 ft (9 145 m); econ cruise, 528 mph (850 km/h) at 39,000 ft (11 885 m); range (with max payload), 3,660 mls (5 890 km), (max fuel), 5,257 mls (8 460 km).

Weights: Operational empty, 126,060 lb (57 180 kg); max take-off (medium range), 230,000 lb (104 325 kg), (long range), 250,000 lb (113 395 kg).

Accommodation: Flight crew of two and nine standard interior arrangements for 178 (16 first and 162 tourist class), 186 (16 first and 170 tourist class), 202 (12 first and 190 tourist class), 208 (12 first and 196 tourist class), or 214, 220, 223, 224 or 239 tourist class passengers.

Status: First Model 757 flown 19 February 1982, with first customer deliveries (to Eastern) on 22 December 1982. Total orders and options were 724 at the beginning of 1991 with more than 300 delivered and production continuing at seven monthly.

Notes: Current variants of the basic Boeing 757 include the 757-200PF (Package Freighter) featuring a large side cargo door in the forward fuselage and a windowless interior, and the 757-200M Combi, which, retaining all passenger windows, has an upward-opening cargo door in the forward fuselage. With RB211-535C engines, the 757-200 allegedly provides a 53 per cent reduction in fuel burn per seat by comparison with the previous-generation medium-haul airliners. The 757-200 was the first airliner to be launched by Boeing with a non-American engine. EROPS (Extended Range Operations) FAA approval over water has been granted with both Rolls-Royce and Pratt & Whitney engines.

BOEING 757-200

Dimensions: Span, 124 ft 10 in (38,05 m); length, 155 ft 3 in (47,32 m); height, 44 ft 6 in (13,56 m); wing area, 1,994 sq ft (185,25 m²).

BOEING 767-300

Country of Origin: USA.

Type: Medium-haul commercial transport.

Power Plant: Two 50,000 lb st (222·4 kN) Pratt & Whitney PW4050 or 52,000 lb st (231·3 kN) PW4052, or 52,500 lb st (233·5 kN) General Electric CF6-80C2B2 turbofans.

Performance: (CF6-80C2B2) Max cruise speed (at 260,000 lb/117 935 kg), 563 mph (906 km/h) at 39,000 ft (11 890 m); range cruise, 529 mph (852 km/h) at 39,000 ft (11 890 m); range (max payload), 3,706 mls (5 965 km), (max fuel) 6,160 mls (9 915 km).

Weights: Operational empty, 184,000 lb (83 461 kg); max take-off, 345,000 lb (156 489 kg).

Accommodation: Flight crew of two (with optional third position) and basic arrangement for 216 passengers comprising 18 first-class six abreast and 198 tourist-class seven abreast. Alternative single-class layouts for 230, 242 and 255 passengers.

Status: First Model 767 flown on 26 September 1981, with first customer delivery (United) following 19 August 1982. First -300 flown on 30 January 1986, with first delivery (JAL) following 25 September. Orders and options (all versions) totalled 526 aircraft at the beginning of 1991, with approximately 400 delivered and production continuing at a rate of five monthly.

Notes: The -300 version of the Boeing 767 differs from the -200 primarily in having a 21·25-ft (6,48-m) fuselage stretch, a strengthened undercarriage and increased-gauge skinning in some areas. Variants include the -300ER extended-range model with optional gross weights of 380,000 lb (172 365 kg) and 387,000 lb (175 540 kg), and the necessary structural changes to accommodate these and increased fuel capacity.

BOEING 767-300

Dimensions: Span, 156 ft 1 in (47,57 m); length, 180 ft 3 in (54,94 m); height, 52 ft 0 in (15,85 m); wing area, 3,050 sq ft (283,3 m²).

BOEING E-3 SENTRY

Country of Origin: USA.

Type: Airborne warning and control system aircraft.

Power Plant: Four (E-3A, B and C) 21,000 lb st (93·4 kN) Pratt & Whitney TF33-PW-100/100A or (E-3D and F) 24,000 lb st (106·76 kN) CFM International CFM56-2A-3 turbofans.

Performance: (E-3A, B and C) Max speed, 530 mph (853 km/h) at 30,000 ft (9 145 m); max continuous cruise, 495 mph (797 km/h) at 29,000 ft (8 840 m); typical loiter speed, 376 mph (605 km/h); max unrefuelled endurance, 11·5 hrs; time on station at 1,000 mls (1 610 km) from base, 6 hrs; ferry range, 5,034 mls (8 100 km) at 475 mph (764 km/h).

Weights: (E-3A) Empty, 170,277 lb (77 238 kg); normal loaded, 214,300 lb (97 206 kg); max take-off, 325,000 lb (147 420 kg).

Accommodation: Basic flight crew of four on flight deck and normal mission crew of 13 systems operators occupying tactical compartments (this number can vary for specific missions).

Status: First of two development aircraft flown 9 February 1972, these and 22 E-3As built for USAF subsequently updated to E-3B standards and redelivered July 1984. Final 10 for USAF (including updated third test aircraft) delivered as E-3Cs. Eighteen E-3As (similar in standard to E-3C) delivered to multinational NATO force 1982–1985. All subsequent Sentries powered by CFM56 engines, these comprising five for Royal Saudi Air Force delivered 1986–87, seven for the RAF (E-3Ds) and four for France's *Armée de l'Air* (E-3Fs) with deliveries having commenced in 1990 and scheduled to be completed during 1991.

Notes: The RAF's E-3D Sentry AEW Mk 1 (illustrated) has additional outboard wing stringers and stiffeners to cater for tip pods and trailing-edge HF antennae.

BOEING E-6A HERMES

Dimensions: Span, 148 ft 2 in (45,16 m); length, 152 ft 11 in (46,61 m); height, 42 ft 5 in (12,93 m); wing area, 3,050 sq ft (283·4 m²).

BRITISH AEROSPACE 146-300

Country of Origin: United Kingdom.
Type: Short-haul commercial transport.
Power Plant: Four 6,970 lb st (31·0 kN) Textron Lycoming ALF502R-5, or (from late 1991) 7,000 lb st (31·13 kN) LF507 turbofans.
Performance: (ALF502R-5 engines) Max cruise speed, 491 mph (789 km/h) at 29,000 ft (8 840 m); long-range cruise, 434 mph (699 km/h) at 29,000 ft (8 840 m); range (standard fuel), 1,750 mls (2 817 km), (max payload), 1,197 mls (1 927 km).
Weights: Operational empty, 54,848 lb (24 878 kg); max take-off, 97,500 lb (44 225 kg).
Accommodation: Flight crew of two and standard seating for 103 passengers five abreast and a maximum of 128 passengers.
Status: Aerodynamic prototype of 146-300 (conversion of first 146-100 prototype) flown on 1 May 1987, with first production Series 300 following in June 1988, orders totalling 58 (including 10 -300QTs) by beginning of 1991 when orders for all versions totalled 263 and production was rising to 40 annually.
Notes: The Series 300 BAe 146 represents the second 'stretch' of the basic design, possessing the same wing and engines as the Series 100 and 200 from which it differs essentially in fuselage length, these being respectively 86 ft 5 in (26,34 m) and 93 ft 10 in (28,60 m). All three Series are available in QT (Quiet Trader) dedicated freighter form and QC quick-change convertible passenger/freighter form, and the Series 100 is offered in RJ70 and RJ80 (see pages 70–71) dedicated regional transport versions. From late 1991, all versions are to be powered by the higher-thrust LF507 turbofan, permitting a 4,000-lb (1 815-kg) increase in the gross weight of the Series 300, a greater payload and a 173-mile (278-km) max payload range increase. Some structural changes are to be introduced simultaneously and new avionics are to be provided.

BRITISH AEROSPACE 146-300

Dimensions: Span, 86 ft 0 in (26,21 m); length, 101 ft 8 in (30,99 m); height, 28 ft 3 in (8,61 m); wing area, 832 sq ft (77,30 m²).

BRITISH AEROSPACE 1000

Country of Origin: United Kingdom.

Type: Corporate executive transport.

Power Plant: Two 5,200 lb st (23·13 kN) Pratt & Whitney Canada PW305 turbofans.

Performance: Max cruise speed, 539 mph (867 km/h) at 29,000 ft (8 840 m); econ cruise, 463 mph (745 km/h) at 39,000–43,000 ft (11 890–13 100 m); time to 35,000 ft (10 670 m), 19 min; service ceiling, 43,000 ft (13 100 m); range (max payload), 3,960 mls (6 375 km), (max fuel with VFR reserves), 4,185 mls (6 736 km).

Weights: Empty, 16,820 lb (97 629 kg); max take-off, 31,000 lb (14 060 kg).

Accommodation: Flight crew of two (with provision for third crew member on flight deck) and (typically) eight passengers in a double 'club-four' arrangement, or one 'club-four' plus three-seat divan and one single seat in main cabin. Up to 15 passengers in 'business express' configuration.

Status: First of two development aircraft flown on 16 June 1990, with second following on 26 November. These were scheduled to be joined early 1991 by first series aircraft leading to certification in the fourth quarter of the year. Orders and commitments for 21 BAe 1000s had been received by the beginning of 1991.

Notes: A long-range, larger-cabin derivative of the BAe 125 (see 1989/90 edition) which remains in parallel production, the BAe 1000 features a 2 ft 9 in (0,84 m) fuselage stretch, new and more powerful engines, a fuel tank in an extended forward wing fairing and increased ventral tank capacity. The re-styled cabin interior offers increased headroom by comparison with that of the BAe 125. Range and field performance are 21 and 15 per cent improved respectively over those of the BAe 125-800.

BRITISH AEROSPACE 1000

Dimensions: Span, 51 ft 4 in (15,66 m); length, 53 ft $10\frac{1}{2}$ in (16,42 m); height, 17 ft 1 in (5,21 m); wing area, 374 sq ft (34,75 m²).

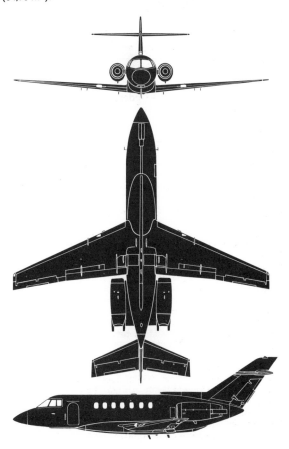

BRITISH AEROSPACE ATP

Country of Origin: United Kingdom.

Type: Regional commercial transport.

Power Plant: Two 2,653 shp (1,978 kW) Pratt & Whitney Canada PW126A turboprops.

Performance: Max cruise speed, 306 mph (493 km/h) at 13,000 ft (3 960 m); econ cruise, 272 mph (437 km/h) at 18,000 ft (5 485 m); range (max payload with reserves), 662 mls (1 065 km), (with 64 passengers and reserves), 1,134 mls (1 825 km).

Weights: Operational empty, 31,290 lb (14 193 kg); max take-off, 50,550 lb (22 930 kg).

Accommodation: Flight crew of two and standard arrangement for 64 passengers four abreast with central aisle, and alternative arrangements for 60 to 72 seats.

Status: Two prototypes flown on 6 August 1986 and 20 February 1987, with certification following in March 1988. The first customer delivery (to British Midland) took place in April 1988, with 39 aircraft ordered by beginning of 1991 when 28 had been delivered and production was running at one aircraft monthly.

Notes: The ATP (Advanced Turboprop) is technically a stretched development of the BAe 748, with new engines, systems and equipment, swept vertical surfaces and a redesigned fuselage nose. It incorporates an advanced flight deck with EFIS (Electronic Flight Instrument System) and is claimed to be the only new-generation turboprop airliner capable of utilising jetways at major airports.

BRITISH AEROSPACE ATP

Dimensions: Span, 100 ft 6 in (30,63 m); length, 85 ft 4 in (26,01 m); height, 23 ft 5 in (7,14 m); wing area, 842·84 sq ft (78,30 m²).

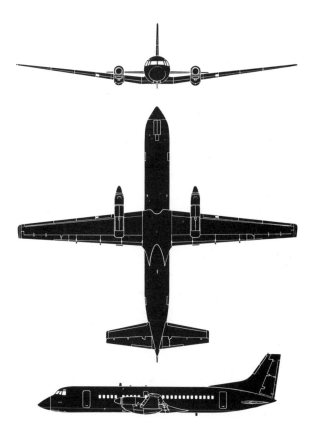

BRITISH AEROSPACE HARRIER GR MK 7

Countries of Origin: United Kingdom and USA.

Type: Single-seat V/STOL close support and tactical reconnaissance aircraft.

Power Plant: One 21,750 lb st (96·75 kN) Rolls-Royce Pegasus Mk 105 vectored-thrust turbofan.

Performance: Max speed, 661 mph (1 065 km/h) at sea level, or Mach = 0·87, 600 mph (966 km/h) at 36,000 ft (10 975 m), or Mach = 0·91; tactical radius (with 12 Mk 82 bombs and one hour loiter), 103 mls (167 km), (HI-LO-HI mission profile with seven Mk 82 bombs and two 250 Imp gal/1 136 l external tanks, but no loiter allowance), 553 mls (889 km); ferry range (max external fuel), 2,015 mls (3 243 km) tanks retained, 2,418 mls (3 891 km) tanks dropped.

Weights: Approx operational empty, 14,000 lb (6 350 kg); max take-off (VTO), 18,950 lb (8 595 kg), (STO), 31,000 lb (14 061 kg).

Armament: Two 25-mm cannon (on under-fuselage stations) and up to 16 Mk 82 or six Mk 83 bombs, six BL-755 cluster bombs, four Maverick ASMs, or 10 rocket pods on six wing stations. Max external load, 9,200 lb (4 173 kg).

Status: First GR Mk 7 (converted GR Mk 5) flown 29 November 1989, and delivery of 34 new-build aircraft to the RAF commencing early 1991. These are to be followed by 58 further GR Mk 7s upgraded from GR Mk 5s.

Notes: The Harrier GR Mk 7 is based on the GR Mk 5 (the RAF equivalent of the US Marine Corps' AV-8B), but has additional equipment for nocturnal and bad weather operations. The GR Mk 7 airframe is built jointly by British Aerospace and McDonnell Douglas on a 50-50 basis, the AV-8B being manufactured on a 40-60 basis. See TAV-8B, pages 158–9.

BRITISH AEROSPACE HARRIER GR MK 7

Dimensions: Span, 30 ft 4 in (9,24 m); length, 46 ft 4 in (14,12 m); height, 11 ft 7¾ in (3,55 m); wing area (including LERX), 238·7 sq ft (22,18 m²).

BRITISH AEROSPACE HAWK 100

Country of Origin: United Kingdom.

Type: Tandem two-seat advanced systems trainer and light ground attack aircraft.

Power Plant: One 5,845 lb st (26·0 kN) Rolls-Royce Turboméca Adour 871 turbofan.

Performance: Max speed, 644 mph (1 037 km/h) at sea level, or Mach = 0·845, 580 mph (933 km/h) at 36,000 ft (10 975 m), or Mach = 0·88; max initial climb, 11,800 ft/min (59,95 m/sec); combat radius (with four 1,000-lb/453,6-kg bombs and gun pod), 148 mls (239 km) LO-LO-LO, 759 mls (1 222 km) HI-LO-HI; combat air patrol (with two Sidewinder AAMs, a 30-mm gun pod and two 190 Imp gal/864 l drop tanks), 2·75 hrs low-altitude loiter 115 mls (185 km) from base.

Weights: Empty, 8,752 lb (3 970 kg); max take-off, 18,739 lb (8 500 kg).

Armament: One 30-mm cannon pod on fuselage centreline and up to six Sidewinder AAMs (four underwing and two at wingtips), or (ground attack) four 1,000-lb (453,6-kg) or eight 500-lb (226,8-kg) bombs and one 30-mm cannon pod.

Status: Aerodynamic prototype (modified from Hawk 60 demonstrator) flown 21 October 1987, second (fully representative) prototype joined flight test programme 1990. First production deliveries (Abu Dhabi) 1991. Orders at the beginning of 1991 comprised 12 for Abu Dhabi, eight for Oman and 10 for Malaysia.

Notes: Basically a two-seater, but designed to carry only a pilot on combat missions, the Hawk 100 series is an enhanced development of the Hawk basic/advanced trainer fitted with a 'combat wing' with manually-selected combat flap, fixed leading-edge droop and other changes to improve manoeuvrability, and wingtip missile launchers.

BRITISH AEROSPACE HAWK 100

Dimensions: Span (including wingtip missles), 32 ft 7⅜ in (9,94 m); length (including probe), 38 ft 11 in (11,86 m); height, 13 ft 8 in (4,16 m); wing area, 179·6 sq ft (16,69 m²).

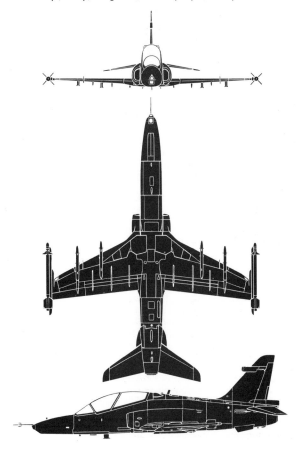

BRITISH AEROSPACE HAWK 200

Country of Origin: United Kingdom.
Type: Single-seat multi-role lightweight fighter.
Power Plant: One 5,845 lb st (26·0 kN) Rolls-Royce Turbo-méca Adour 871 turbofan.
Performance: Max speed, 644 mph (1 037 km/h) at sea level, or Mach = 0·845; econ cruise, 495 mph (796 km/h) at 41,000 ft (12 500 m); max initial climb, 11,510 ft/min (58,47 m/sec); range (internal fuel), 554 mls (892 km), (with max external fuel), 2,244 mls (3 610 km).
Weights: Empty, 9,100 lb (4 127 kg); max take-off, 20,065 lb (9 101 kg).
Armament: One or two internally-mounted 25-mm Aden cannon and up to five Sidewinder AAMs, or (close air support) up to five 1,000-lb (453,6-kg) and four 500-lb (226,8-kg) bombs. Each underwing pylon capable of lifting 2,000 lb (907 kg) within the maximum external load of 7,700 lb (3 493 kg).
Status: First prototype flown on 19 May 1986, with first pre-production aircraft following on 24 April 1987, and production-standard demonstrator due to fly early 1991. Production orders at the beginning of 1991 comprised eight for Oman and 18 for Malaysia.
Notes: A private venture single-seat combat version of the Hawk trainer, the Hawk 200 series is virtually identical with the two-seat Hawk 100 series aft of the cockpit, giving 80 per cent airframe commonality. The avionics fit and 'combat wing' are similar to those of the Hawk 100.

BRITISH AEROSPACE HAWK 200

Dimensions: Span (including wingtip missiles), 32 ft 7$\frac{3}{8}$ in (9,94 m); length, 37 ft 4 in (11,38 m); height, 13 ft 8 in (4,16 m); wing area, 179·6 sq ft (16,69 m²).

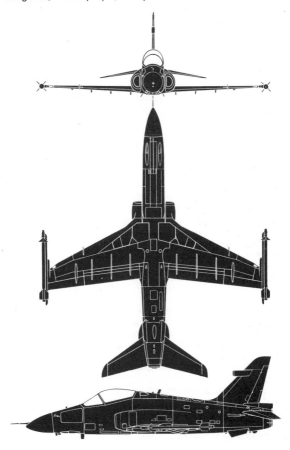

BRITISH AEROSPACE JETSTREAM 41

Country of Origin: United Kingdom.
Type: Light regional commercial transport.
Power Plant: Two 1,500 shp (1,118 kW) Garrett TPE331-14GR/HR turboprops.
Performance: (Estimated) Max cruise speed, 340 mph (547 km/h) at 20,000 ft (6 100 m); econ cruise, 299 mph (482 km/h) at 20,000 ft (6 100 m); max initial climb, 2,200 ft/min (11,18 m/sec); service ceiling, 26,000 ft (7 925 m); range (29 passengers and IFR reserves), 680 mls (1 095 km).
Weights: Operational empty (typical), 13,544 lb (6 144 kg); max take-off, 22,377 lb (10 150 kg).
Accommodation: Flight crew of two and up to 29 or (with galley) 27 passengers three abreast.
Status: First of three aircraft for flight development (to be delivered to customers subsequently) scheduled to fly early summer 1991, with customer deliveries commencing in the autumn of 1992. Fifteen to be delivered during 1992, with 25 following in 1993 and 35 in 1994. Ten orders plus 60 options held by beginning of 1991.
Notes: The Jetstream 41 has been derived from the Jetstream Super 31 (see 1989/90 edition) from which it differs primarily in having a lengthened fuselage with improved cabin access and a longer-span wing mounted lower on the fuselage. A rearward-extended wingroot fairing affords additional baggage space. More than 350 Jetstream 31s and Super 31s had been ordered by the beginning of 1991.

BRITISH AEROSPACE JETSTREAM 41

Dimensions: Span, 60 ft 0 in (18,29 m); length, 63 ft 2 in (19,25 m); height, 18 ft 10 in (5,74 m); wing area, 350·8 sq ft (32,59 m²).

BRITISH AEROSPACE RJ70/80

Country of Origin: United Kingdom.
Type: Short-haul regional airliner.
Power Plant: Four 7,000 lb st (31·13 kN) Textron Lycoming LF507 turbofans (derated approximately 10 per cent).
Performance: Max cruise speed (for 575-mile/925-km sector), 477 mph (767 km/h) at 29,000 ft (8 840 m); range cruise, 416 mph (669 km/h); range (RJ70), 920 mls (1 480 km) with 70 passengers and reserves, (RJ80), 980 mls (1 575 km) with 80 passengers and reserves.
Weights: Max take-off (RJ70), 80,000 lb (36 288 kg), (RJ80), 84,000 lb (38 100 kg).
Accommodation: Flight crew of two and seating (typical) for (RJ70) 70 passengers five abreast, or (RJ80) 80 passengers six abreast.
Status: RJ70 concept aircraft (modified BAe 146-100) demonstrated from autumn 1990, with first series model to fly third quarter of 1991 and deliveries (to Comair) anticipated for 1992. Orders for 10 (plus options on further 10) being negotiated at the beginning of 1991.
Notes: The RJ70 and RJ80, respectively aimed at the North American and European markets, are derivatives of the BAe 146 Series 100 'optimised' for the newly-defined regional jet transport requirement. Differing essentially in accommodation, both RJ70 and RJ80 will have the new LF507 turbofan, which, available from late 1991, offers increased thrust at higher temperatures, but is being derated for installation in these commuter aircraft to afford improved life and economy. Lightweight versions of the basic BAe 146 Series 100, their weights being linked to the shorter ranges required for the type of operation for which they are intended, the low first cost of the BJ70 and BJ80 is linked to a minimum-size order.

BRITISH AEROSPACE RJ70/80

Dimensions: Span, 86 ft 0 in (26,21 m); length, 85 ft 11½ in (26,20 m); height, 28 ft 3 in (8,61 m); wing area, 832 sq ft (77,30 m²).

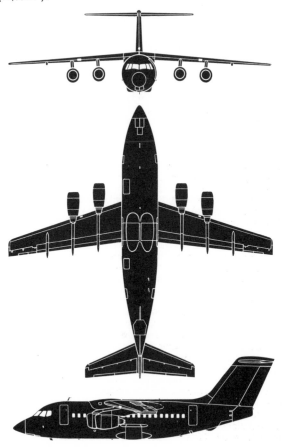

BRITISH AEROSPACE SEA HARRIER
FRS MK 2

Country of Origin: United Kingdom.
Type: Single-seat V/STOL shipboard multi-role fighter.
Power Plant: One 21,500 lb st (95·6 kN) Rolls-Royce Pegasus 106 vectored-thrust turbofan.
Performance: Max speed, 720 mph (1 160 km/h) at 1,000 ft (305 m), or Mach=0·95, 607 mph (977 km/h) at 36,000 ft (10 975 m), or Mach=0·92, (with two Martel ASMs and two AIM-9L AAMs), 598 mph (962 km/h) at sea level, or Mach= 0·83; combat radius (high altitude intercept with 3 min combat) 480 mls (750 km), (surface attack with two Sea Eagle AShMs and two 30-mm cannon), 230 mls (370 km).
Weights: Approx operational empty, 14,500 lb (6 577 kg); max take-off, 26,500 lb (12 020 kg).
Armament: External fuselage packs for two 25-mm or 30-mm cannon, or two AIM-120 AAMs on fuselage stations, plus two stores stations under each wing for free-fall or retarded 1,000-lb (453,6-kg) bombs, cluster bombs, 68-mm rocket packs, AIM-9L or AIM-120 AAMs, Sea Eagle AShMs, or ALARM anti-radiation missiles.
Status: The first of two development FRS Mk 2s was flown on 19 September 1988. At the beginning of 1991, 29 FRS Mk 1s were being rotated through an upgrade programme to FRS Mk 2 standard and 10 new-build FRS Mk 2s were on order for the Royal Navy.
Notes: The Sea Harrier FRS Mk 2 differs from the current FRS Mk 1 in having a Blue Vixen pulse-Doppler radar providing 'lookdown/shootdown' capability, a redesigned cockpit, improved systems and the ability to carry up to four AIM-120 AMRAAMs. The aft fuselage is lengthened by 1 ft 1¾ in (35 cm).

BRITISH AEROSPACE SEA HARRIER FRS MK 2

Dimensions: Span, 25 ft 3 in (7,70 m); length, 46 ft 3 in (14,10 m); height, 12 ft 2 in (3,71 m).

CANADAIR CL-215T

Country of Origin: Canada.
Type: Multi-purpose amphibian.
Power Plant: Two 2,380 shp (1 775 kW) Pratt & Whitney Canada PW123AF turboprops.
Performance: Max cruise speed (at 32,500 lb/14 741 kg), 234 mph (376 km/h) at 10,000 ft (3 050 m); range cruise, 178 mph (287 km/h); patrol speed (at 35,000 lb/15 876 kg), 127 mph (204 km/h) at sea level; max initial climb (at 46,000 lb/20 865 kg), 1,280 ft/min (6,5 m/sec); ferry range, 1,295 mls (2 085 km).
Weights: Operational empty (utility), 25,990 lb (11 789 kg), (water bomber), 26,550 lb (12 043 kg); max take-off (land), 43,850 lb (19,890 kg), (water), 37,700 lb (17 100 kg); max flying weight (after water scooping), 46,000 lb (20 865 kg).
Accommodation: Normal flight crew of two with additional stations for flight engineer, navigator and two observers for maritime surveillance duties, or 32–35 passengers in transport configuration. Maximum disposable payload of 13,500 lb (6 123 kg) as a water bomber or 10,560 lb (4 790 kg) in utility configuration.
Status: Two CL-215T prototypes (converted from CL-215s) were flown on 8 June and 20 September 1989, with retrofit kits for conversion of existing aircraft to CL-215T standard becoming available during 1990. The Quebec Government is the launch customer for the conversion, other customers including the Spanish government for 15 conversion kits. At the beginning of 1991, the French Government was negotiating for 12 new-build CL-215Ts with deliveries commencing 1993.
Notes: One hundred and twenty-five piston-engined CL-215s were built with production terminating April 1990. The new-build CL-215T will have powered controls and (in water bomber version) a new four-door, four-tank water drop system.

CANADAIR CL-215T

Dimensions: Span, 93 ft 10 in (28,60 m); length, 65 ft $0\frac{1}{4}$ in (19,82 m); height (on land), 29 ft $5\frac{1}{2}$ in (8,98 m); wing area, 1,080 sq ft (100,33 m²).

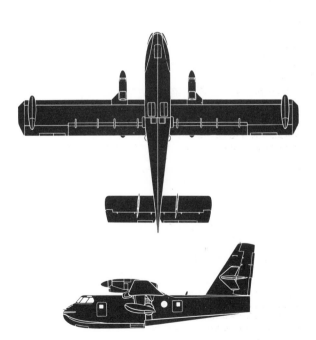

CANADAIR REGIONAL JET

Country of Origin: Canada.
Type: Regional transport.
Power Plant: Two 8,729 lb st (38·83 kN) or 9,220 lb st (41·0 kN) (with automatic power reserve) General Electric CF34-3AI turbofans.
Performance: (Manufacturer's estimates) Max cruise speed, 529 mph (851 km/h) at 36,000 ft (10 975 m), or Mach = 0·80; long-range cruise, 488 mph (786 km/h) at 36,000 ft (10 975 m), or Mach = 0·74; max initial climb, 3,900 ft/min (19,8 m/sec); time to 35,000 ft (10 670 m), 23 min; range (max payload), 973 mls (1 566 km); extended range, 1,633 mls (2 628 km).
Weights: Manufacturer's empty, 29,180 lb (13 236 kg); max take-off, 47,450 lb (21 523 kg), or (extended-range option), 51,000 lb (23 133 kg).
Accommodation: Flight crew of two and standard cabin layout for 50 passengers four abreast.
Status: First pre-production aircraft scheduled to fly in April 1991, with second and third joining the flight development programme before the year's end. Initial customer deliveries (to DLT) to commence in 1992. By the beginning of 1991, firm orders had been placed for 23 aircraft with options covering a further 22, and 94 aircraft were covered by memoranda of understanding.
Notes: The Regional Jet, or RJ, is a derivative of the Challenger (see 1989–90 edition) embodying fuselage extensions of 10 ft 8 in (3,25 m) forward of the wing and 9 ft 4 in (2,84 m) aft, an increase of some 15 per cent in wing area, and various other changes to translate the aircraft from light corporate executive transport to regional airliner. The basic 50-seater is referred to as the Series 100 and the extended-range model as the Series 100-ER.

CANADAIR REGIONAL JET

Dimensions: Span, 70 ft 4 in (21,44 m); length, 88 ft 5 in (26,95 m); height, 20 ft 8 in (6,30 m); wing area, 520 sq ft (48,31 m²).

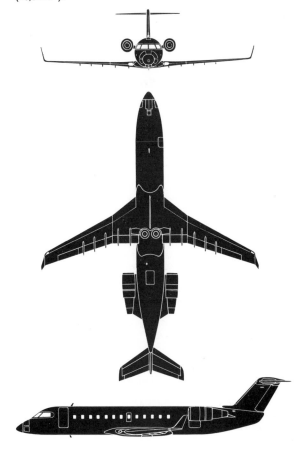

CASA C-212-300 AVIOCAR

Country of Origin: Spain.
Type: Commercial and military STOL utility transport.
Power Plant: Two 900 shp (671 kW) Garrett TPE331-10R-513C turboprops.
Performance: Max cruise speed, 220 mph (354 km/h) at 10,000 ft (3 050 m); econ cruise, 186 mph (300 km/h) at 10,000 ft (3 050 m); max initial climb, 1,630 ft/min (8,28 m/sec); service ceiling, 26,000 ft (7 925 m); range (25 passengers and IFR reserves), 273 mls (440 km) at max cruise, (with 3,776-lb/1 713-kg payload), 890 mls (1 433 km).
Weights: Empty equipped (cargo), 9,700 lb (4 400 kg); max take-off, 16,975 lb (7 700 kg), (military), 17,637 lb (8 000 kg).
Accommodation: Flight crew of two and standard seating for up to 26 passengers three abreast, 25 inward-facing seats for 24 paratroops and jumpmaster, or 25 fully-equipped troops, or 12 stretcher patients and four medical attendants.
Status: The current production model of the Aviocar, the C-212-300, was first flown in 1985, and certificated in December 1987, replacing the -200 (the standard version from 1979). Some 450 C-212s (all versions) had been delivered by the beginning of 1991, when licence manufacture by IPTN in Indonesia was continuing.
Notes: The Srs 300 differs from preceding versions of the Aviocar primarily in having a lengthened nose, semi-winglets on a longer-span wing, some structural modifications and upgraded avionics. The military C-212-300M has been supplied to the air forces of Angola, Bolivia, France and Panama, and maritime patrol versions have been supplied to the Argentine coastguard.

CASA C-212-300 AVIOCAR

Dimensions: Span, 66 ft 6½ in (20,28 m); length, 52 ft 11¾ in (16,15 m); height, 21 ft 7¾ in (6.60 m); wing area, 441·33 sq ft (41,00 m²).

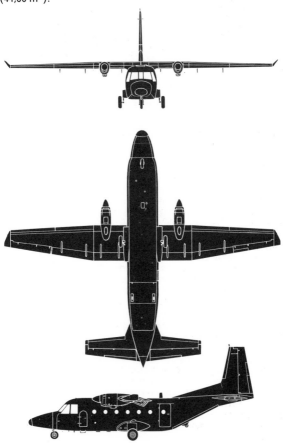

CESSNA MODEL 208 (U-27A) CARAVAN I

Country of Origin: USA.

Type: Light commercial and military (U-27A) utility and special missions aircraft.

Power Plant: One 600 shp (447 kW) Pratt & Whitney Canada PT6A-114 turboprop.

Performance: (Model 208B) Max cruise speed, 197 mph (317 km/h) at 10,000 ft (3 050 m), 183 mph (295 km/h) at 20,000 ft (6 095 m); max initial climb, 770 ft/min (3,9 m/sec); service ceiling, 21,900 ft (6 675 m); max range (with 45 min reserves), 1,108 mls (1 783 km) at 10,000 ft (3 050 m), 1,242 mls (2 000 km) at 18,000 ft (5 485 m).

Weights: (Model 208B) Standard empty, 4,570 lb (2 073 kg); max take-off, 8,750 lb (3 969 kg).

Accommodation: Pilot and (Model 208) up to nine passengers or 3,000 lb (1 360 kg) of freight, or (Model 208B) 3,500 lb (1 587 kg) of freight in standard configuration, or nine to (with FAR Pt 23 waiver) 14 passengers.

Status: Engineering prototype of Model 208 flew on 9 December 1982, with customer deliveries commencing in February 1985, a military version (U-27A) being introduced in 1986. The Model 208B flew in prototype form on 3 March 1986. At the beginning of 1991, deliveries were continuing against Federal Express orders for 249 aircraft (including 210 of the Model 208B version), an option on a further 100 being held. Some 470 Caravan Is (all versions) had been delivered by January 1991 when production was 7–8 monthly.

Notes: The U-27A (illustrated above) and Model 208B (opposite page) are respectively military and stretched (by 4 ft/ 1.22 m) versions of the basic Model 208.

CESSNA MODEL 208B CARAVAN I

Dimensions: Span, 52 ft 1 in (15,87 m); length, 41 ft 7 in (12,67 m); height, 14 ft 10 in (4,52 m); wing area, 279·4 sq ft (25,96 m²).

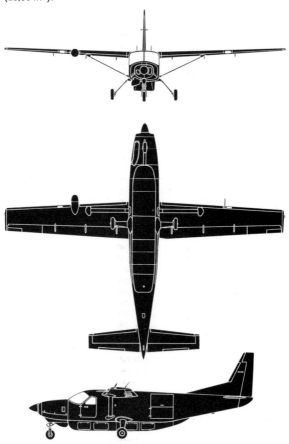

CESSNA MODEL 525 CITATIONJET

Country of Origin: USA.

Type: Light corporate executive transport.

Power Plant: Two 1,900 lb st (8·6 kN) Williams International FJ44 turbofans.

Performance: (Manufacturer's estimates) Max cruise (at 8,500 lb/3 856 kg), 440 mph (708 km/h) at 33,000 ft (10 060 m), 423 mph (680 km/h) at 39,000 ft (11 885 m); long-range cruise, 317 mph (510 km/h) at 29,000 ft (8 840 m), 355 mph (570 km/h) at 39,000 ft (11 885 m); max altitude, 41,000 ft (12 495 m); range (four passengers and 45 min reserves), 1,727 mls (2 780 km).

Weights: Empty, 5,730 lb (2 599 km); max take-off, 10,000 lb (4 536 km).

Accommodation: Pilot and co-pilot/passenger on flight deck and standard main cabin arrangement for five passengers in two forward- and two aft-facing seats, and one side-facing seat.

Status: First prototype CitationJet scheduled to enter flight test during May 1991, with second prototype following six months later. FAA certification is anticipated in October 1992 with customer deliveries commencing in the following December.

Notes: Intended successor to the Citation I, production of which terminated in 1985, the CitationJet retains the forward fuselage structure of the Citation II which it mates with a new wing, new rear fuselage and T-type tail. The wing section has been developed in conjunction with Boeing and NASA.

CESSNA MODEL 525 CITATIONJET

Dimensions: Span, 45 ft 2½ in (13,78 m); length, 42 ft 7¼ in (12,98 m); height, 13 ft 8½ in (4,18 m); wing area, 240 sq ft (22,30 m²).

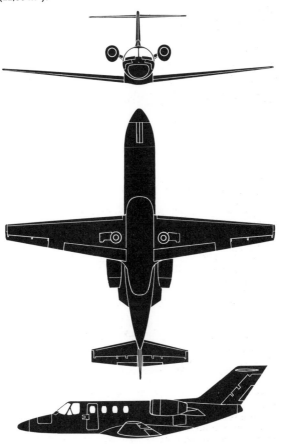

CESSNA MODEL 560 CITATION V

Country of Origin: USA.

Type: Light corporate executive transport.

Power Plant: Two 2,900 lb st (12·89 kN) Pratt & Whitney Canada JT15D-5A turbofans.

Performance: Max cruise speed, 492 mph (791 km/h) at 33,000 ft (10 060 m); max initial climb, 3,650 ft/min (18,54 m/sec); max operating altitude, 45,000 ft (13 700 m); range (six passengers with VFR reserves and allowances), 2,211 mls (3 558 km) at high speed cruise.

Weights: Standard empty, 8,950 lb (4 060 kg); max take-off, 15,900 lb (7 212 kg).

Accommodation: Pilot and co-pilot/passenger on flight deck and standard arrangements for eight passengers in centre or double-club seating.

Status: Engineering prototype of the Citation V flown on 18 August 1987, a pre-production prototype joining the development programme early 1988, and FAA certification being awarded on the following 9 December, with the first customer delivery in April 1989.

Notes: A development of the Model 550 Citation S/II, the Citation V has a stretched fuselage, an additional window in each side of the cabin and uprated engines. The US Navy operates 15 Citation S/IIs as T-47As for training personnel in the use of air-to-air, air-to-surface, intercept and other radar equipment.

CESSNA MODEL 560 CITATION V

Dimensions: Span, 52 ft 2½ in (15,90 m); length, 48 ft 10¾ in (14,90 m); height, 15 ft 0 in (4,57 m); wing area, 342·6 sq ft (31,83 m²).

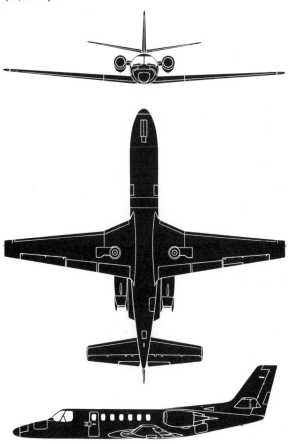

DASSAULT ATLANTIQUE 2 (ATL 2)

Country of Origin: France.
Type: Long-range maritime patrol aircraft.
Power Plant: Two 6,100 ehp (4,549 kW) Rolls-Royce Tyne RTy 20 Mk 21 turboprops.
Performance: Max speed, 402 mph (648 km/h) at optimum altitude, 368 mph (592 km/h) at sea level; max continuous cruise, 345 mph (586 km/h) at 25,000 ft (7,620 m); normal patrol speed, 195 mph (315 km/h) at 5,000 ft (1 525 m); max initial climb (at 88,185 lb/40 000 kg), 2,000 ft/min (10,1 m/sec); patrol time (basic mission), 8 hrs at 690 mls (1 112 km) from base, 5 hrs at 1,150 mls (1 850 km) from base; ferry range, 5,635 mls (9 075 km).
Weights: Empty equipped, 56,217 lb (25 500 kg); normal loaded weight, 97,443 lb (44 200 kg); max take-off, 101,852 lb (46 200 kg).
Accommodation: Normal flight crew of 10 comprising two pilots, two flight engineer/observers, one mission tactical co-ordinator and five systems operators.
Armament: Up to eight Mk 46 homing torpedoes, nine 550-lb (250-kg) bombs, or 12 depth charges and two AM 39 Exocet ASMs. Four underwing stations for up to 7,716 lb (3 500 kg) of stores.
Status: First of two prototypes (converted ATL 1s) flown 8 May 1981, and first series ATL 2 flown 19 October 1988. First acceptance by *Aéronavale* on 26 October 1989, with total requirement for 42 aircraft of which 22 ordered with increments of three being ordered annually.
Notes: The Atlantique 2 (ATL 2) is a modernised version of the ATL 1, production of which ended in 1973 after 87 series aircraft had been built. The Italian Navy is upgrading its ATL 1s with ATL 2 weapons systems.

DASSAULT ATLANTIQUE 2 (ATL 2)

Dimensions: Span, 122 ft 9¼ in (37,42 m); length, 103 ft 9 in (31,62 m); height, 35 ft 8¾ in (10,89 m); wing area, 1,295·3 sq ft (120,34 m²).

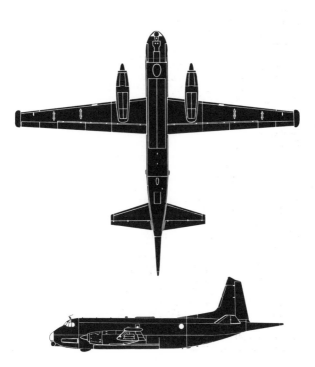

DASSAULT FALCON 900

Country of Origin: France.
Type: Light corporate executive transport.
Power Plant: Three 4,500 lb st (20 kN) Garrett TFE731-5AR-1C turbofans.
Performance: Max speed (at 27,000 lb/12 250 kg), 574 mph (924 km) at 36,000 ft (10 975 m), or Mach = 0·87; max cruise, 554 mph (892 km/h) at 39,000 ft (11 890 m), or Mach = 0·84; econ cruise, 495 mph (797 km/h) at 37,000 ft (11 275 m), or Mach = 0·75; range (max payload and IFR reserves), 3,984 mls (6 412 km), (with 15 passengers), 4,329 mls (6 968 km), (with eight passengers), 4,491 mls (7 227 km).
Weights: Operational empty (typical) 23,248 lb (10 545 kg); max take-off, 45,500 lb (20 640 kg).
Accommodation: Flight crew of two and optional main cabin arrangements for 8–15 passengers, with maximum seating layout for 18 passengers three abreast.
Status: Two prototypes flown on 21 September 1984 and 30 August 1985, with first customer delivery following on 19 December 1986 and some 90 aircraft delivered by the beginning of 1991.
Notes: The Falcon 900 is the largest member of the Mystère-Falcon family of corporate executive transports and has been adopted by several countries (Australia, France, Malaysia, Nigeria and Spain) for governmental transportation tasks. Two examples of a maritime surveillance version serve with the Japanese Maritime Safety Agency. The Falcon 2000, scheduled to enter flight test early in 1993, is based on the Falcon 900 fuselage cross section shortened by a third and powered by two GE/Garrett CFE738 engines. Possessing considerable commonality with the 900, the 2000 will replace the 20 and 200 series Falcons.

DASSAULT FALCON 900

Dimensions: Span, 63 ft 5 in (19,33 m); length, 66 ft $3\frac{2}{3}$ in (20,21 m); height, 24 ft $9\frac{1}{4}$ in (7,55 m); wing area, 527·77 sq ft (49,03 m²).

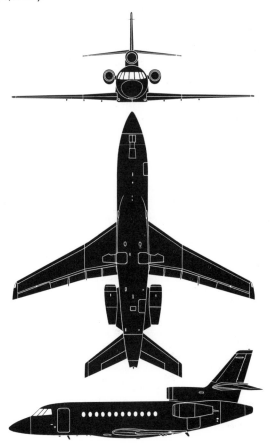

DASSAULT MIRAGE 2000D

Country of Origin: France.
Type: Tandem two-seat deep penetration interdictor and strike aircraft.
Power Plant: One 14,460 lb st (64·3 kN) dry and 21,385 lb st (95·1 kN) SNECMA M53-P2 turbofan.
Performance: Max speed (short endurance dash), 1,485 mph (2 390 km/h) above 36,090 ft (11 000 m), or Mach = 2·25, (continuous), 1,386 mph (2 230 km/h), or Mach = 2·1, (low altitude with eight 551-lb/250-kg bombs and two Magic 2 AAMs), 695 mph (1 118 km/h), or Mach = 0·912; max initial climb, 59,055 ft/min (300 m/sec); range (with max external fuel), 2,073 mls (3 335 km); tactical radius (two 374 Imp gal/1 700 l drop tanks and 2,205-lb/1 000-kg external ordnance plus two Magic 2 AAMs), 930 mls (1 500 km).
Weights: Empty equipped, 17,085 lb (7 750 kg); loaded (clean), 23,800 lb (10 800 kg); max take-off, 38,140 lb (17 300 kg).
Armament: Fuselage centreline and inboard wing stations each stressed for 3,968 lb (1 800 kg), plus four fuselage stations each stressed for 882 lb (400 kg) and two outboard wing stations each stressed for 661 lb (300 kg). Up to 13,228 lb (6 000 kg) of ordnance plus two Magic 2 self-defence AAMs.
Status: Mirage 2000D conventional attack derivative of the Mirage 2000N, the first of two prototypes which flew on 3 February 1983. Planning at the beginning of 1991 called for 105 2000Ds (plus 75 2000Ns) of which 57 (75) funded.
Notes: The 2000N (illustrated above) is optimised for the medium-range nuclear missile-carrying role and the 2000S is an export equivalent of the 2000D.

DASSAULT MIRAGE 2000D

Dimensions: Span, 29 ft 11½ in (9,13 m); length, 47 ft 9 in (14,55 m); height, 16 ft 10¾ in (5,15 m); wing area, 441·3 sq ft (41,00 m²).

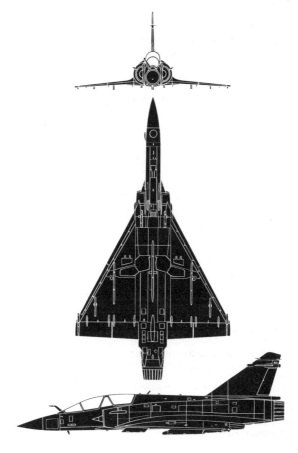

DASSAULT RAFALE C

Country of Origin: France.

Type: Single-seat interceptor and multi-role fighter.

Power Plant: Two 10,950 lb st (48·7 kN) dry and 16,400 lb st (72·9 kN) afterburning SNECMA M88-2 turbofans.

Performance: (Estimated) Max speed, 1,320 mph (2 124 km/h) above 36,000 ft (10 975 m), or Mach=2·0, 920 mph (1 480 km/h) at low altitude, or Mach=1·2; tactical radius (air-to-air mission with eight Mica AAMs and one 374 Imp gal/1 700 l centreline and two 286 Imp gal/1 300 l underwing drop tanks), 1,152 mls (1 853 km), (HI-LO-LO-HI penetration with 12 551-lb/250-kg bombs, four Mica AAMs and 946 Imp gal/4 300 l external fuel), 679 mls (1 093 km).

Weights: Empty equipped, 19,973 lb (9 060 kg); max take-off, 42,990 lb (19 500 kg).

Armament: One 30-mm cannon and normal external ordnance load (on 14 attachment points) of 13,228 lb (6 000 kg), with maximum permissible load of 17,637 lb (8 000 kg).

Status: First prototype Rafale C was scheduled to enter flight test in March 1991, with navalised Rafale M prototype following before end of 1991 and first Rafale B two-seat prototype flying in 1993. Current planning calls for 225 Rafale Cs and 25 Bs for the *Armée de l'Air* and 86 Rafale Ms for the *Aéronavale*, production deliveries being scheduled to commence 1996.

Notes: The Rafale C is a production derivative of the Rafale A advanced fighter technology demonstrator (see 1989/90 edition). It is about three per cent smaller than its predecessor, has larger movable canards, replaces some carbon composites with superplastic-formed diffusion-bonded titanium construction and has an empty weight trimmed by approximately 1,100 lb (500 kg).

DASSAULT RAFALE C

Dimensions: Span (including wingtip missiles), 35 ft $9\frac{1}{8}$ in (10,90 m); length, 50 ft $2\frac{1}{3}$ in (15,30 m); wing area, 484·39 sq ft (45,00 m²).

DE HAVILLAND CANADA DASH 8-300A

Country of Origin: Canada.
Type: Regional commercial transport.
Power Plant: Two 2,380 shp (1,775 kW) Pratt & Whitney Canada PW123 turboprops.
Performance: Max cruise speed (at 40,850 lb/18 530 kg), 330 mph (531 km/h) at 15,000 ft (4 575 m), 325 mph (523 km/h) at 20,000 ft (6 100 m); range (50 passengers with IFR reserves), 1,250 mls (2 012 km).
Weights: Operational empty, 25,700 lb (11 657 kg); max take-off, 41,100 lb (18 643 kg), optional, 43,000 lb (19 505 kg).
Accommodation: Flight crew of two and up to 56 passengers four abreast with single aisle. Standard arrangement for 50 passengers.
Status: Dash 8-300 prototype (converted from Dash 8-100) flown on 15 May 1987, with first customer delivery (to Time Air) following 27 February 1989, and first Dash 8-300A high gross weight version (to Contact Air) on 24 August 1990. All subsequent aircraft featuring the higher gross weight option. Orders (all versions) totalled 351 aircraft at the beginning of 1991 with 241 delivered.
Notes: The Dash 8-300 series is a stretched version of the original -100 series with fore and aft plugs totalling 11 ft 3 in (3,43 m), increased wing span, a strengthened undercarriage and more powerful engines. Development was continuing during 1990 of a further stretch of the basic design, the -400 seating up to 70 passengers and cruising at 404 mph (650 km/h). The -400 was on hold at the beginning of 1991. The Dash 8 has proved itself amenable to adaptation for wide range of missions. Two Dash 8M-100s serve as passenger/cargo transports with the Canadian Armed Forces as CC-142s and four others are operated as CT-142 navigational trainers. Two serve with the USAF as E-9A missile range control aircraft, these being equipped as flying data links simultaneously transmitting data and performing radar surveillance functions.

DE HAVILLAND CANADA DASH 8-300A

Dimensions: Span, 90 ft 0 in (27,43 m); length, 84 ft 3 in (25,68 m); height, 24 ft 7 in (7,49 m); wing area, 605 sq ft (56,21 m²).

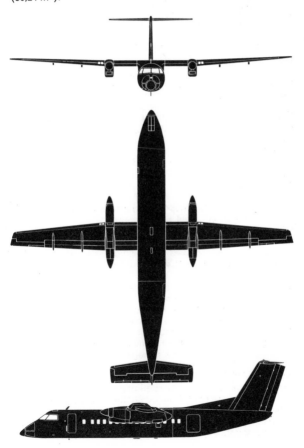

DEUTSCHE AEROSPACE (DORNIER) 228-200

Country of Origin: Germany.

Type: Light regional and utility transport, medevac and maritime patrol aircraft.

Power Plant: Two 715 shp (533 kW) Garrett TPE331-5-A-252D turboprops.

Performance: (228-212) Max cruise speed, 266 mph (428 km/h) at 10,000 ft (3 050 m), 230 mph (370 km/h) at sea level; range cruise, 253 mph (408 km/h) at 15,000 ft (4 575 m); econ cruise, 207 mph (333 km/h); max initial climb, 1,870 ft/min (9,5 m/sec); range (with 19 passengers and reserves), 725 mls (1 167 km), (with 1,708-lb/775-kg payload), 1,520 mls (2 446 km) at max range speed.

Weights: (228-212) Operational empty, 8,249 lb (3 742 kg); max take-off, 14,110 lb (6 400 kg) increasable to 14,550 lb (6 600 kg) in special cases.

Accommodation: Flight crew of one or two and 19–20 passengers. Standard cabin arrangement comprising 14 individual seats with central aisle, two paired seats and three seats along rear bulkhead.

Status: Prototype 228-100 flown 28 March 1981, with prototype -200 following on 9 May. Customer deliveries commenced February 1982, with approximately 190 (all versions) delivered by beginning of 1991 from Dornier Luftfahrt production when manufacturing rate was 1·5–2·0 monthly. Licence manufacture in progress in India of up to 150 228-101s and -201s.

Notes: The Do 228-212 is the current production version of the basic light transport, having been certificated in Germany in 1989, and in France and the USA in 1990. This offers increased range and improved take-off performance, increased take-off weight being catered for by strengthened wing, fuselage and undercarriage. By comparison with the -100 series, the -200 series has a lengthened fuselage. Three specialised maritime patrol versions of the -200 have been developed, together with signal intelligence and reconnaissance models.

DEUTSCHE AEROSPACE (DORNIER) 228-200

Dimensions: Span, 55 ft 7 in (16,97 m); length, 54 ft 4 in (16,56 m); height, 15 ft 9 in (4,86 m); wing area, 344·46 sq ft (32,00 m²).

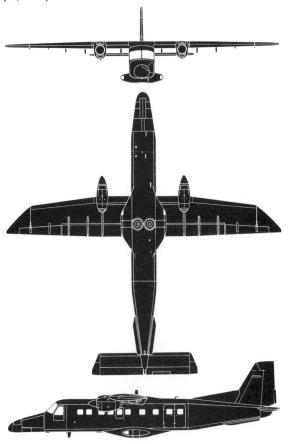

DEUTSCHE AEROSPACE (DORNIER) 328

Country of Origin: Germany.
Type: Light regional commercial transport.
Power Plant: Two 2,180 shp (1 627 kW) Pratt & Whitney Canada PW119 turboprops.
Performance: (Estimated) Max cruise speed, 398 mph (640 km/h) at 25,000 ft (7 620 m); max initial climb, 2,430 ft/min (12,34 m/sec); service ceiling, 31,000 ft (9 450 m); range (30 passengers and allowances for 115-mile/185-km diversion and 45 min hold), 808 mls (1 300 km), (16 passengers), 1,727 mls (2 780 km).
Weights: Max take-off, 27,557 lb (12 500 kg).
Accommodation: Flight crew of two and 30–33 passengers three abreast, with maximum seating for 39 passengers four abreast.
Status: First flight scheduled for July 1991, with European JAR certification late 1992, followed by FAA certification early 1993. First delivery (to Contactair) late 1992, and to USA (Midway Commuter) first quarter 1993. Orders and options totalled approximately 100 aircraft at beginning 1991.
Notes: The Do 328, developed by the Dornier Luftfahrt subsidiary of Deutsche Aerospace, retains the basic wing profile of the smaller Do 228, with an enlarged centre section and new flap system, combining this with a new, larger circular-section fuselage. Offering short take-off and landing characteristics, the Do 328 can operate from rough, unprepared strips. Current planning includes a stretched version, the Do 328L, with 48-seat capacity, a corporate executive transport version (for which the first order had been placed by the beginning of 1991), civil and military freighters, and a surveillance version. The Do 328 is the first commercial aircraft to feature a composite (Kevlar and carbonfibre-reinforced plastic) pressure bulkhead.

DEUTSCHE AEROSPACE (DORNIER) 328

Dimensions: Span, 68 ft 10 in (20,98 m); Length, 69 ft $7\frac{1}{2}$ in (21,22 m); height, 23 ft $7\frac{1}{2}$ in (7,20 m).

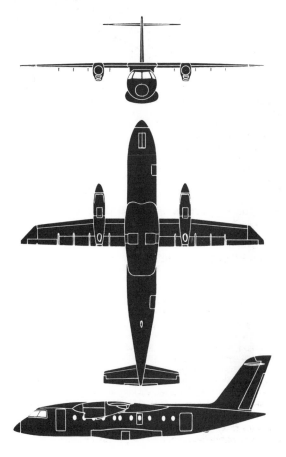

DORNIER COMPOSITE SEASTAR CD2

Country of Origin: Germany.

Type: Light utility amphibian.

Power Plant: Two 650 shp (485 kW) Pratt & Whitney Canada PT6A-135A turboprops.

Performance: Max cruise speed, 219 mph (352 km/h) at 9,840 ft (3 000 m); max initial climb, 1,575 ft/min (8,0 m/sec); service ceiling, 28,215 ft (8 600 m); range (with 12 passengers and 10 per cent reserves), 253 mls (407 km), (with 1,000-lb/454-kg payload), 1,044 mls (1 680 km) at max cruise at 10,000 ft (3 050 m).

Weights: Empty equipped, 5,291 lb (2 400 kg); max take-off, 10,141 lb (4 600 kg).

Accommodation: Flight crew of one or two and maximum of 12 passengers three abreast with single aisle. Alternative arrangements for six passengers in corporate executive transport layout, or six stretcher cases plus two attendants in medevac layout.

Status: First prototype flown 17 August 1984, and two pre-series aircraft following on 24 April 1987 and in October 1988. German type certification obtained 30 September 1990, and first production delivery scheduled for December 1991, with eight being delivered in 1992 and 25 in 1993.

Notes: The Seastar is of all-composite construction, built mainly of glassfibre with carbonfibre reinforcement in the wing spar caps and highly stressed areas. Suitable for operation from water, ice, snow and grass surfaces, the Seastar is claimed to be suitable for a wide variety of commercial and military roles, these including search and rescue, law enforcement, EEZ surveillance and maritime patrol. At the beginning of 1991, Dornier Composite Aircraft GmbH had received letters of intent for 48 of the Seastar.

DORNIER COMPOSITE SEASTAR CD2

Dimensions: Span, 58 ft 4¾ in (17,80 m); length, 40 ft 10½ in (12,46 m); height (on land), 15 ft 1 in (4,60 m); wing area, 329·38 sq ft (30,60 m²).

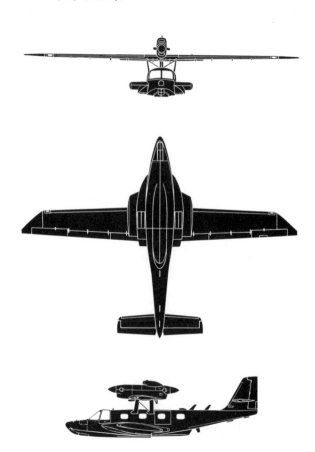

EMBRAER EMB-120 BRASILIA

Country of Origin: Brazil.

Type: Short-haul regional transport.

Power Plant: Two 1,800 shp (1,342 kW) Pratt & Whitney Canada PW118A turboprops.

Performance: Max speed, 378 mph (608 km/h) at 20,000 ft (6 100 m); max cruise, 357 mph (574 km/h) at 25,000 ft (7 620 m); max initial climb, 2,120 ft/min (10,77 m/sec); service ceiling, 32,000 ft (9 755 m); range (with 30 passengers), 576 mls (925 km).

Weights: Operational empty, 15,664 lb (7 105 kg); max take-off, 25,353 lb (11 500 kg).

Accommodation: Flight crew of two and standard arrangements for 30 passengers in three-abreast seating. Also available are a mixed-traffic version for 24 or 26 passengers, an all-cargo version and an executive transport version.

Status: First of three prototypes was flown on 27 July 1983, with first customer delivery following in August 1985, and 200th delivered five years later, in August 1990. Production of 51 Brasilias during 1990 is scheduled to increase to 72 during 1991 at the beginning of which year 316 were on firm order and 177 more on option.

Notes: Embraer's 'second generation' twin-turboprop, the Brasilia achieved FAA type approval on 9 July 1985, and has since been the best-selling aircraft in its category. Apart from corporate and regional transport versions, the Brasilia is offered for a variety of military roles and four have been delivered as VC-97 VIP transports to the Brazilian Air Force which has ordered a further eight as personnel and freight transports. A shortened version of the Brasilia fuselage is used by the CBA-123 Vector, and a lengthened version is currently proposed for the projected EMB-145 45–48 seat regional airliner, configurational design of which was being finalised at the beginning of 1991.

EMBRAER EMB-120 BRASILIA

Dimensions: Span, 64 ft 10¾ in (19,78 m); length, 65 ft 7½ in (20,00 m); height, 20 ft 10 in (6,35 m); wing area, 424·42 sq ft (39,43 m²).

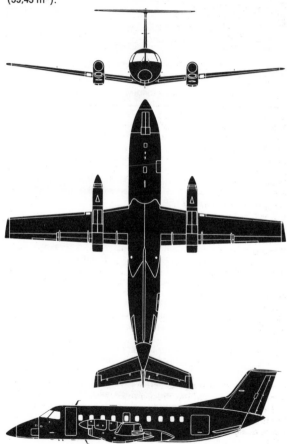

EMBRAER/FMA CBA-123 VECTOR

Countries of Origin: Brazil and Argentina.

Type: Light regional airliner and corporate transport.

Power Plant: Two 1,300 shp (969 kW) Garrett TPF351-20 turboprops.

Performance (Manufacturer's estimates): Max cruise speed, 404 mph (650 km/h) at 24,000 ft (7 315 m); max initial climb, 2,550 ft/min (12,95 m/sec); service ceiling, 36,400 ft (11 095 m); range (19 passengers and IFR reserves), 898 mls (1 445 km), (max fuel), 1,900 mls (3 060 km).

Weights: Operational empty, 13,327 lb (6 045 kg); max take-off, 19,841 lb (9 000 kg).

Accommodation: Flight crew of two and standard commuter arrangement for 19 passengers (plus flight attendant) three abreast with four seats on rear cabin bulkhead.

Status: First of five prototypes (including structural and fatigue test specimens) flown (in Brazil) on 18 July 1990, with second (also in Brazil) following December 1990, and third (in Argentina) early 1991. Certification is anticipated November 1991, and the launching of series production was, at the beginning of 1991, dependent on firm orders for a minimum of 20 aircraft.

Notes: The Vector is being developed jointly by Embraer (80 per cent) in Brazil and FMA (20 per cent) in Argentina, each company planning final assembly lines without component manufacturing duplication. Innovative in having its turboprops pylon-mounted on the rear fuselage and driving six-bladed pusher propellers, the Vector utilises a shortened version of the EMB-120 Brasilia fuselage. Its manufacturers hope to gain 30 per cent of the calculated 2,000-aircraft market for 19-seaters between 1992 and 2005.

EMBRAER/FMA CBA-123 VECTOR

Dimensions: Span, 58 ft 1 in (17,72 m); length, 59 ft 5 in (18,09 m); height, 19 ft 7 in (5,97 m); wing area, 292·79 sq ft (27,20 m²).

EMBRAER EMB-312 TUCANO

Country of Origin: Brazil.
Type: Tandem two-seat basic trainer.
Power Plant: One 750 shp (559 kW) Pratt & Whitney Canada PT6A-25C turboprop.
Performance: (At 5,622 lb/2 550 kg) Max speed, 278 mph (448 km/h) at 10,000 ft (3 050 m); max cruise, 255 mph (411 km/h); econ cruise, 198 mph (319 km/h); max initial climb, 2,331 ft/min (11,84 m/sec); service ceiling, 30,000 ft (9 150 m); range (max internal fuel and 30 min reserves), 1,145 mls (1 844 km) at 20,000 ft (6 100 m); ferry range (with two 145 Imp gal/660 l underwing tanks), 2,069 mls (3 330 km).
Weights: Basic empty, 3,991 lb (1 810 kg); max take-off, 5,622 lb (2 550 kg), (with external stores), 7,000 lb (3 175 kg).
Armament: (Light strike and weapons training) Up to 2,205 lb (1 000 kg) of ordnance distributed between four wing stations.
Status: First of four prototypes flown on 15 August 1980, with deliveries (to the Brazilian Air Force) following from September 1983. Orders placed (and fulfilled) by the beginning of 1991 comprised Argentina (30), Brazil (128), Egypt (54), Honduras (12), Iraq (80), Iran (25), Paraguay (6), Peru (20) and Venezuela (31). In addition, licence manufacture is being undertaken in the UK (see pages 192–3) and a contract for 85 aircraft (including options) for France was being finalised. Production was suspended in 1990, but was expected to be resumed during 1991.
Notes: The parent company was actively pursuing development of a more powerful version of the Tucano at the beginning of 1991.

EMBRAER EMB-312 TUCANO

Dimensions: Span, 36 ft 6½ in (11,14 m); length, 32 ft 4¼ in (9,86 m); height, 11 ft 7⅞ in (3,40 m); wing area, 208·82 sq ft (19,40 m²).

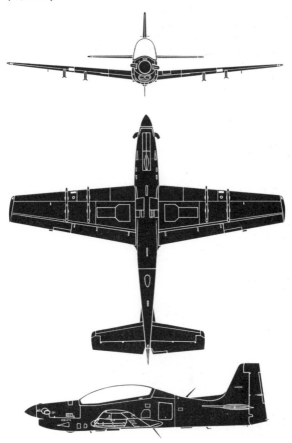

ENAER T-35T TURBO PILLAN

Country of Origin: Chile.

Type: Tandem two-seat primary/basic trainer.

Power Plant: One 420 shp (313 kW) Allison 250-B17D turboprop.

Performance: (At 3,007 lb/1 364 kg) Max speed, 228 mph (367 km/h) at sea level; max continuous cruise (75% power), 214 mph (344 km/h) at 9,840 ft (3 000 m); max initial climb, 2,110 ft/min (10,7 m/sec); service ceiling, 24,850 ft (7 575 m).

Weights: Empty equipped, 2,310 lb (1 048 kg); max take-off, 3,007 lb (1 364 kg).

Armament: (Training and light attack) Two 250-lb (113,4-kg) bombs, two 12,7-mm machine gun pods, or two pods each containing seven 68-mm rockets.

Status: Prototype Turbo Pillán (converted by Soloy from the fourth prototype Pillán) was first flown on 12 February 1986 as the Aucán (Blithe Spirit). Development temporarily suspended for financial reasons, but resumed in 1990 when contract placed with Soloy for conversion kits to convert the Chilean Air Force's fleet of 60 piston-engined Pilláns to Turbo Pillán standard commencing mid 1991. One single-seat Turbo Pillán prototype, the T-35TS, was flown in 1989 as a potential conversion trainer and light attack aircraft.

Notes: The Turbo Pillán is a derivative of the piston-engined Pillán of which 80 (60 T-35As and 20 T-35Bs with avionics for IFR tuition) were built for the Chilean Air Force, four (T-35D) were delivered to the Panamanian Air Force and 40 (T-35C) were assembled by CASA in Spain from ENAER-supplied kits.

ENAER T-35T TURBO PILLAN

Dimensions: Span, 28 ft 11 in (8,81 m); length, 27 ft 2⅓ in (8,29 m); height, 7 ft 8⅛ in (2,35 m); wing area, 147·34 sq ft (13,69 m²).

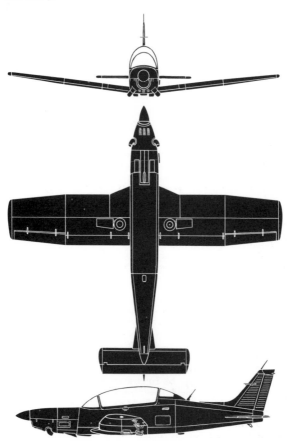

FFT EUROTRAINER 2000

Country of Origin: Germany.

Type: Side-by-side two-seat primary/basic trainer and two-plus-two-seat touring aircraft.

Power Plant: One 270 hp (201 kW) Textron Lycoming AEIO-540-L six-cylinder horizontally-opposed engine.

Performance: (Manufacturer's estimates) Max cruise speed, 201 mph (324 km/h) at sea level; econ cruise (65% power), 181 mph (291 km/h); initial climb, 1,338 ft/min (6,80 m/sec); service ceiling, 20,000 ft (6 095 m).

Weights: Empty, 2,028 lb (920 kg); max take-off (aerobatic), 2,866 lb (1 300 kg), (utility), 3,263 lb (1 480 kg).

Accommodation: Seats for two or four persons in pairs under one-piece hinged canopy.

Status: The first prototype Eurotrainer 2000 was scheduled to enter flight test early 1991, and the first of eight aircraft ordered for Swissair's civil aviation flying school is expected to be delivered early 1992.

Notes: The Eurotrainer 2000, which is built entirely of composite materials, was originally developed by the FFA Flugzeugwerke Altenrhein AG (formerly Flug-und Fahrzeugwerke AG) which transferred all its aviation activities to the Gesellschaft für Flugzeug-und Faserverbund Technologie (FFT) of Mengen, Germany. Originally to have been powered by the 245 hp Porsche PFM 3200 engine and now to have the Lycoming AEIO-540-L, as above, the Eurotrainer 2000 is intended for *ab initio* tuition, screening, navigational instruction and basic aerobatic training, and is stressed for +6 *g* and −3·5 *g*. The design makes provision for the introduction of an additional pair of seats for the utility role. The highly stressed components of the glassfibre airframe are reinforced with carbonfibre.

FFT EUROTRAINER 2000

Dimensions: Span, 34 ft 1½ in (10,40 m); length, 26 ft 6⅞ in (8,10 m); height, 10 ft 6 in (3,20 m); wing area, 150·7 sq ft (14,00 m²).

FMA IA 63 PAMPA

Country of Origin: Argentina.
Type: Tandem two-seat basic/advanced trainer.
Power Plant: One 3,500 lb st (15·57 kN) Garrett TFE731-2-2N turbofan.
Performance: Max speed, 509 mph (819 km/h) at 22,965 ft (7 000 m), 469 mph (755 km/h) at sea level; max cruise, 464 mph (747 km/h) at 13,125 ft (4 000 m); max initial climb, 5,950 ft/min (30,23 m/sec); service ceiling, 43,325 ft (12 900 m); range, 932 mls (1 500 km) at 345 mph (556 km/h) at 13,125 ft (4 000 m).
Weights: Empty, 6,219 lb (2 821 kg); max take-off, 11,023 lb (5 000 kg).
Armament: (Armament training or light attack) One 30-mm cannon pod on fuselage centreline. Max ordnance load (including cannon) of 2,557 lb (1 160 kg) distributed between centreline and four wing stations.
Status: First of three prototypes flown on 6 October 1984, and first three series aircraft delivered to Argentine Air Force on 15 March 1988, with further 15 delivered by beginning of 1991, and additional 50 aircraft programmed by the service.
Notes: Developed on behalf of the Argentine government by the German Dornier concern, the IA 63 is manufactured by the Fabrica Militar de Aviones. The FMA has linked with the LTV Corporation to submit a 'missionised' version of this aircraft as a contender in the JPATS (US Air Force and US Navy Joint Primary Aircraft Training System) contest as the Pampa 2000. The formal flight evaluation of the Pampa 2000 is scheduled to take place in 1994.

FMA IA 63 PAMPA

Dimensions: Span, 31 ft $9\frac{1}{2}$ in (9,69 m); length, 35 ft $9\frac{1}{4}$ in (10,90 m); height, 14 ft $0\frac{3}{4}$ in (4,29 m); wing area, 168·24 sq ft (15,63 m^2).

FOKKER 50

Country of Origin: Netherlands.
Type: Regional commercial transport.
Power Plant: Two 2,500 shp (1,864 kW) Pratt & Whitney Canada PW125B turboprops.
Performance: Max cruise speed, 330 mph (532 km/h) at 20,000 ft (6 100 m); range cruise, 282 mph (454 km/h); max operating altitude, 25,000 ft (7 620 m); range (with 50 passengers and 45 min reserves), 776 mls (1 249 km), (at optional high gross weight), 1,754 mls (2 822 km).
Weights: Operational empty (typical), 27,602 lb (12 520 kg); max take-off (standard), 43,982 lb (19 950 kg), (optional), 45,900 lb (20 820 kg).
Accommodation: Flight crew of two and standard arrangement for 50 passengers four abreast, with optional high-density seating for 58 passengers.
Status: First of two prototypes (based on F27 airframes) flown on 28 December 1985, with first customer delivery (to DLT) following on 7 August 1987. Firm orders and options for 146 aircraft by beginning of 1991, with production rate scheduled to be 34 aircraft during year compared with 37 in 1990, with some 95 delivered.
Notes: Based on the F27-500 Friendship airframe, the Fokker 50 embodies significant design and structural changes, retaining only 20 per cent component commonality with the earlier aircraft. The 2,750 shp (2 050 kW) PW127 engine has been adopted for the 'hot and high' version of the Fokker 50 launched in 1990, and is to be used for the 66-passenger stretched -200 development.

FOKKER 50

Dimensions: Span, 95 ft 1¾ in (29,00 m); length, 82 ft 10 in (25,25 m); height, 27 ft 3½ in (8,32 m); wing area, 753·5 sq ft (70,00 m²).

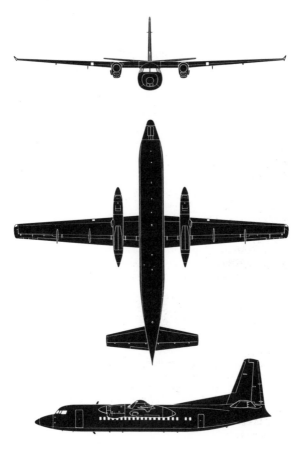

FOKKER 100

Country of Origin: Netherlands.

Type: Short- to medium-haul commercial transport.

Power Plant: Two 13,850 lb st (61·6 kN) Rolls-Royce Tay 620-15 or 15,100 lb st (67·2 kN) Tay 650-15 turbofans.

Performance: Max cruise speed, 535 mph (861 km/h) at 24,200 ft (7 375 m); range cruise, 465 mph (748 km/h) at 35,000 ft (10 670 m); range (Tay 620 with 107 passengers), 1,543 mls (2 483 km), (Tay 650), 1,836 mls (2 956 km).

Weights: Operational empty (Tay 620), 53,738 lb (24 375 kg), (Tay 650), 54,103 lb (24 541 kg); max take-off (Tay 620), 95,000 lb (43 090 kg), (Tay 650), 98,000 lb (44 450 kg).

Accommodation: Flight crew of two and standard arrangement for 107 passengers five abreast. Optional layouts include 12 first-class and 85 economy-class four and five abreast respectively, or 55 business- and 50 economy-class all five abreast.

Status: First of two prototypes flown 30 November 1986, with first customer delivery (to Swissair) following on 25 February 1987. Total of 237 on firm order (plus 136 on option) at the beginning of 1991, with 50 delivered and production rising to 67 annually by 1993.

Notes: Technically a derivative of the F28 Fellowship, the Fokker 100 makes extensive use of advanced technology, has new systems and equipment, new engines, a lengthened fuselage and aerodynamically redesigned wings. A higher gross weight version (101,000 lb/45 800 kg) is planned for delivery from early 1993 with Tay 650s and integral centre wing tank (in place of current bag tanks), and a stretched version for up to 135 passengers and powered by Tay 680s is offered.

FOKKER 100

Dimensions: Span, 92 ft 1½ in (28,08 m); length, 116 ft 6¾ in (35,53 m); height, 27 ft 10½ in (8,60 m); wing area, 1,006·4 sq ft (93,50 m²).

GENERAL DYNAMICS F-16 FIGHTING FALCON

Country of Origin: USA.

Type: Single-seat multi-role fighter and (A-16) close air support and battlefield air interdiction aircraft.

Power Plant: One 23,770 lb st (105·7 kN) with afterburning Pratt & Whitney F100-PW-220 or 28,984 lb st (128·9 kN) General Electric F110-GE 100 turbofan.

Performance: (At 27,245 lb/12 356 kg with F100 engine) Max speed (short endurance dash), 1,333 mph (2 145 km/h) at 40,000 ft (12 190 m), or Mach=2·02, (sustained), 1,247 mph (2 007 km/h), or Mach=1·89; tactical radius (HI-LO-HI interdiction on internal fuel with six 500-lb/227-kg bombs), 360 mls (580 km); ferry range (max external fuel), 2,450 mls (3 943 km).

Weights: Empty, 18,238 lb (8 273 kg); normal loaded (air-to-air mission), 26,463 lb (12 000 kg); max take-off (with max external load), 42,300 lb (19 187 kg).

Armament: One 20-mm rotary cannon and up to 12,430 lb (5 638 kg) of ordnance and fuel distributed between one fuselage centreline and six underwing stations, plus wingtip stations for AAMs.

Status: First of two (YF-16) prototypes flown 20 January 1974. Approximately 2,200 F-16s delivered by parent company (plus a further 510 from European assembly lines) by the beginning of 1991 when production was continuing at a rate of 15 aircraft monthly.

Notes: In late 1990 it was decided to retrofit between 300 and 400 F-16C and two-seat F-16D (Block 30) aircraft for the close air support role as A-16s. Two hundred and seventy earlier F-16As and Bs have been modified as air defence fighters for the Air National Guard.

GENERAL DYNAMICS F-16 FIGHTING FALCON

Dimensions: Span (over missile launchers), 31 ft 0 in (9,45 m); length, 49 ft 4 in (15,03 m); height, 16 ft 8½ in (5,09 m); wing area, 300 sq ft (27,87 m²).

GRUMMAN E-2C HAWKEYE

Country of Origin: USA.

Type: Shipboard or shore-based airborne early warning, surface surveillance and strike control aircraft.

Power Plant: Two 4,910 shp (3,661 kW) Allison T56-A-425 or 5,250 shp (3,915 kW) T56-A-427 turboprops.

Performance: (-425 engines at 51,933 lb/23 556 kg) Max speed, 372 mph (598 km/h); max cruise, 358 mph (576 km/h); max initial climb, 2,515 ft/min (12,8 m/sec); service ceiling, 30,800 ft (9 390 m); time on station (200 mls/320 km from base), 3–4 hrs; ferry range, 1,604 mls (2 580 km).

Weights: Empty, 38,063 lb (17 265 kg); max take-off, 51,933 lb (23 556 kg).

Accommodation: Normal flight crew of two and (main compartment) combat information centre officer, air control officer and radar operator.

Status: First of two E-2C prototypes flown 20 January 1971, with first production aircraft following on 23 September 1972. Approximately 120 delivered to US Navy by the beginning of 1991 against planned total procurement of 144. Four supplied to Israel, eight to Japan (with five more on order), six to Egypt and four to Singapore. The US Coast Guard and US Customs Service have two each.

Notes: Evolved from the E-2A (56 of which were built with 52 upgraded to E-2B standard), the E-2C differs fundamentally in supplanting the 'blue water' capable APS-96 radar with APS-120 capable of target detection and tracking over land. The improved AP-138 was retrofitted from 1983, and this gave place to the AP-139 in new-build E-2Cs from 1988. From 1990, these radars were supplanted, in turn, by the APS-145 with extended detection range and improved overland clutter resistance.

GRUMMAN E-2C HAWKEYE

Dimensions: Span, 80 ft 7 in (24,56 m); length, 57 ft 7 in (17,55 m); height, 18 ft 4 in (5,69 m); wing area, 700 sq ft (65,03 m²).

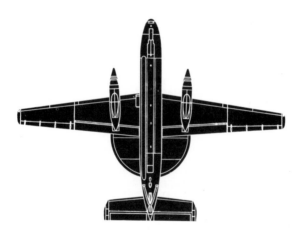

GRUMMAN F-14D TOMCAT

Country of Origin: USA.

Type: Two-seat multi-role shipboard fighter.

Power Plant: Two 14,000 lb st (62·3 kN) dry and 23,100 lb st (102·75 kN) reheat General Electric F110-GE-400 turbofans.

Performance: Max speed (with four semi-recessed AIM-7 AAMs), 1,544 mph (2 485 km/h) at 40,000 ft (12 190 m), or Mach = 2·34, 912 mph (1 468 km/h) at sea level, or Mach = 1·2; intercept radius (at Mach = 1·3), 510 mls (820 km); combat air patrol loiter time (with external fuel), 2·7 hrs.

Weights: (Estimated) Empty, 42,000 lb (19 050 kg); max take-off, 75,000 lb (34 020 kg).

Armament: One 20-mm rotary cannon and (typical) four AIM-54C Phoenix (beneath fuselage) or AIM-7 Sparrow (semi-recessed) AAMs, plus four AIM-9 Sidewinder short-range AAMs or two additional Phoenix or Sparrow missiles on fixed-glove pylons.

Status: First new-build F-14D flown March 1990, with 12 delivered by beginning of 1991 when 25 more were on order and production line scheduled to close 1993. Remanufacturing programme to bring F-14A to similar standards as F-14D(R) initiated June 1990, with six aircraft (four at Grumman and two at Naval Aircraft Depot) having entered programme by year's end and first scheduled to be completed September 1991. Programme to re-manufacture additional aircraft terminated February 1991.

Notes: The F-14D represents the second stage in a two-stage upgrade of the F-14A of which 557 delivered to US Navy. The first stage was the F-14A(Plus) which, retaining essentially similar systems to the F-14A, is re-engined with the F110. The first prototype F-14A(Plus) flew on 29 September 1986, with the first of 38 new-build examples following on 14 November 1987, and last being delivered early 1990, 32 F-14As being converted to the same standard. The F-14D has some 60 per cent new avionics, including APG-71 radar, ASN-139 digital navigation and JTIDS secure datalink.

GRUMMAN F-14D TOMCAT

Dimensions: Span (20 deg sweep), 64 ft 1½ in (19,55 m), (68 deg sweep), 38 ft 2½ in (11,65 m); length, 62 ft 8 in (19,10 m); height, 16 ft 0 in (4,88 m); wing area, 565 sq ft (52,49 m²).

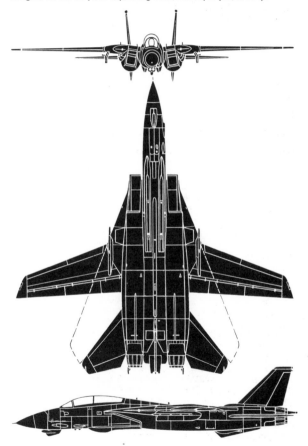

GULFSTREAM AEROSPACE GULFSTREAM IV

Country of Origin: USA.

Type: Long-range corporate executive transport.

Power Plant: Two 13,850 lb st (61·6 kN) Rolls-Royce Tay Mk 611-8 turbofans.

Performance: Max cruise speed, 586 mph (943 km/h) at 31,000 ft (9 450 m); normal cruise, 528 mph (850 km/h) at 45,000 ft (13 715 m); max initial climb, 4,000 ft/min (20,32 m/ sec); range (max fuel and eight passengers, and IFR reserves), 4,859 mls (7 820 km), (with max payload and IFR reserves), 4,254 mls (6 845 km).

Weights: Empty, 35,500 lb (16 102 kg); max take-off, 73,200 lb (33 203 kg).

Accommodation: Flight crew of two or three and standard seating for 14 to 19 passengers.

Status: First of four production prototypes flown on 19 September 1985, with FAA certification being granted on 22 April 1987. Total of 160 Gulfstream IVs delivered by the beginning of 1991 when production tempo was being reduced from 30 to 24 aircraft annually.

Notes: The Gulfstream IV is an advanced version of the Gulfstream III, differing primarily in having a structurally redesigned wing incorporating 30 per cent fewer parts, more internal fuel capacity, a lengthened fuselage, a longer-span tailplane and uprated engines. Several military versions of the Gulfstream IV are on offer, including the SRA-4 multi-role special missions aircraft (see 1989/90 edition). Its tasks include electronic warfare support, surveillance (in which it can fly 9·24 hours on station at 33,000–47,000 ft/10 060–14 325 m) and maritime patrol (six hours on station at 528 mls/850 km from base). In February 1988, a Gulfstream IV performed an eastbound around-the-world flight for which it was awarded eleven records.

GULFSTREAM AEROSPACE GULFSTREAM IV

Dimensions: Span, 77 ft 10 in (23,72 m); length, 88 ft 4 in (26,90 m); height, 24 ft 10 in (7,60 m); wing area, 950·39 sq ft (88,29 m²).

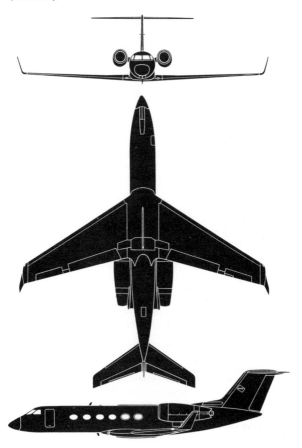

IAR-99 SOIM

Country of Origin: Romania.
Type: Tandem two-seat basic/advanced trainer and light ground attack aircraft.
Power Plant: One 4,000 lb st (17·79 kN) Turbomecanica-built Rolls-Royce Viper 632-41M turbojet.
Performance: Max speed, 537 mph (865 km/h) at sea level; max initial climb, 6,890 ft/min (35 m/sec); service ceiling, 42,320 ft (12 900 m); max endurance (trainer), 2·66 hrs, (ground attack), 1·48 hrs; max range (trainer), 683 mls (1 100 km), (ground attack), 601 mls (967 km).
Weights: Empty equipped, 7,055 lb (3 200 kg); normal loaded (trainer), 9,700 lb (4 400 kg); max take-off (ground attack), 12,257 lb (5 560 kg).
Armament: (Weapons training and ground attack) One 23-mm GSh-23L cannon in fuselage centreline pod. Four under-wing stores stations stressed for 661 lb (300 kg) inboard and 441 lb (200 kg) outboard. Typical weapons loads include two 551-lb (250-kg) and two 220-lb (100-kg) bombs, four multiple carriers each with three 110-lb (50-kg) bombs, or two similar multiple carriers plus two 16×57-mm L-57-16MD rocket launchers.
Status: The first prototype was flown on 21 December 1985, with first deliveries to the Romanian Air Force in 1989 against initial contract for 50 aircraft. Twenty-seven delivered by the beginning of 1991. Option on a further 100 aircraft.
Notes: The Soim (Falcon) is manufactured by the IAv Craiova (Craiova Aircraft Enterprise) primarily as a replacement for the Czechoslovak L 29 Delfin trainer in Romanian Air Force service, but it is also to be utilised by the service for the close air support task if current options are translated into firm orders.

IAR-99 SOIM

Dimensions: Span, 32 ft $3\frac{3}{4}$ in (9,85 m); length, 36 ft $1\frac{1}{2}$ in (11,01 m); height, 12 ft $9\frac{1}{2}$ in (3,90 m); wing area, 201·4 sq ft (18,71 m²).

ILYUSHIN IL-76 (CANDID)

Country of Origin: USSR.

Type: Heavy-duty medium- and long-haul military and commercial freighter, and (Il-78) flight refuelling tanker.

Power Plant: Four 26,455 lb st (117·7 kN) MKB (Soloviev) D-30KP turbofans.

Performance: (Il-76T) Max speed, 528 mph (850 km/h) at 32,810 ft (10 000 m); max continuous cruise, 497 mph (800 km/h) at 42,650 ft (13 000 m); normal cruise altitude, 29,500–39,370 ft (9 000–12 000 m); range at 374,780 lb (170 000 kg) with 45 min reserves, 1,864 mls (3 000 km) with 103,615-lb (47 000-kg) payload, 4,040 mls (6 500 km) with 44,090-lb (20 000-kg) payload.

Weights: Max take-off, 374,780 lb (170 000 kg).

Accommodation: Normal crew of seven (including two freight handlers). Modules available for quick configuration changes each able to accommodate 30 passengers in four-abreast seating, casualty stretchers or cargo. Three such modules may be carried.

Status: First of four prototypes flown on 25 March 1971, with first of 25 pre-series aircraft following early 1975, these being delivered to both Aeroflot (Il-76T) and the SovAF (Il-76M). By beginning of 1991, when production was continuing at a rate of four aircraft monthly, some 450 Il-76s were serving with the SovAF and more than 120 with Aeroflot. Nearly 100 civil and military Il-76s have been exported.

Notes: Progressive developments of the commercial Il-76T and military Il-76M with increased weights have been the Il-76TD and MD. A three-point flight refuelling tanker essentially similar to the Il-76MD is the Il-78 (Midas) illustrated above, and an airborne early warning and control version (see 1989/90 edition) with saucer radome has the reporting name Mainstay.

ILYUSHIN IL-76 (CANDID)

Dimensions: Span, 165 ft 8⅓ in (50,50 m); length, 152 ft 10¼ in (46,59 m); height, 48 ft 5¼ in (14,76 m); wing area, 3,229·2 sq ft (300,00 m²).

ILYUSHIN IL-96-300

Country of Origin: USSR.
Type: Long-haul commercial transport.
Power Plant: Four 35,275 lb st (156·9 kN) Perm (Soloviev) PS-90A turbofans.
Performance: (Manufacturer's estimates) Max cruise speed, 559 mph (900 km/h) at 39,700 ft (12 100 m); econ cruise, 528 mph (850 km/h) at 33,135 ft (10 100 m); range (with reserves and max payload), 4,660 mls (7 500 km), (with reserves and 66,140-lb/30 000-kg payload), 5,592 mls (9 000 km), (with reserves and 33,070-lb/15 000-kg payload), 6,835 mls (11 000 km).
Weights: Basic operational, 257,936 lb (117 000 kg); max take-off, 476,200 lb (216 000 kg).
Accommodation: Flight crew of three and basic all-economy class arrangement for 300 passengers nine abreast in two cabins. Various optional arrangements including a 235-seat mixed-class version with 22 first-class passengers six abreast, 40 business-class passengers eight abreast and 173 economy-class passengers basically nine abreast.
Status: The first of three flying prototypes was flown on 28 September 1988, the second and third following in 1989 and 1990 respectively. Initial customer deliveries (to Aeroflot) are expected spring 1991, and current planning calls for 60–70 Il-96s (possibly including Il-96Ms) prior to completion of the current five-year programme in 1995.
Notes: Possessing a superficial resemblance to the earlier Il-86, the Il-96 is fundamentally a new design. A stretched version, the Il-96-350 capable of accommodating 350 passengers, is scheduled to fly in 1993, and a twin-engined variant, the Il-96M powered by Pratt & Whitney PW2037 turbofans, is expected to enter flight test in 1992–93.

ILYUSHIN IL-96-300

Dimensions: Span (excluding winglets), 189 ft 2 in (57,66 m); length, 181 ft 7¼ in (55,35 m); height, 57 ft 7¾ in (17,57 m); wing area, 4,215 sq ft (391·6 m²).

ILYUSHIN IL-114

Country of Origin: USSR.
Type: Regional commercial transport.
Power Plant: Two 2,368 shp (1,766 kW) Leningrad KB (Isotov) TV7-117 turboprops.
Performance: (Estimated) Max cruise speed, 310 mph (500 km/h) at 26,740 ft (8 150 m); optimum cruise altitude, 19,685–26,250 ft (6 000–8 000 m); range with reserves (with 11,905 lb/5 400-kg payload), 621 mls (1 000 km), (with 7,935-lb/3 600-kg payload), 1,770 mls (2 850 km), (with 3,300-lb/1 500-kg payload), 2,980 mls (4 800 km).
Weights: Operational empty, 30,200 lb (13 700 kg); max take-off, 46,296 lb (21 000 kg).
Accommodation: Flight crew of two and basic arrangement for 60 passengers seated four abreast with central aisle.
Status: First prototype flown on 29 March 1990, with production deliveries scheduled to commence in 1992. To be assembled at Tashkent with some components being contributed by Poland, Romania and Bulgaria, the Il-114 is to be manufactured in large numbers, production of some 500 being envisaged during the 1990–95 five-year plan.
Notes: Intended as a successor to the Antonov An-24 in Aeroflot service, the Il-114 bears a striking resemblance to the British Aerospace ATP. Intended to operate over Aeroflot internal routes of up to 620 miles (1 000 km) in length, the Il-114 makes extensive use of composite materials and advanced metal alloys, including titanium, in its structure, and is intended to operate from both paved and grass surfaces. An optional feature of the aircraft will be large carry-on baggage shelves in a lobby by the main door at the front of the main cabin. Preliminary plans have been announced for the development of a stretched version for 70–75 passengers.

Dimensions: Span, 98 ft 5¼ in (30,00 m); length, 86 ft 3⅔ in (26,31 m); height, 30 ft 7 in (9,32 m).

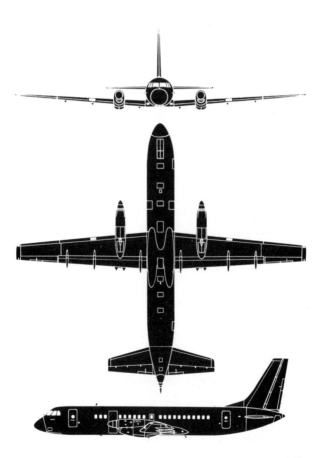

LEARJET 60

Country of Origin: USA.

Type: Light corporate executive transport.

Power Plant: Two 4,400 lb st (19,8 kN) Pratt & Whitney Canada PW305 turbofans.

Performance: Max speed, 549 mph (884 km/h) at 30,000 ft (9 150 m), or Mach = 0·81; max operating altitude, 51,000 ft (15 550 m); max range (at long-range power at 44,000 ft/ 13 410 m with VFR reserves), 3,155 mls (5 075 km); typical range (four passengers and IFR reserves), 2,475 mls (3 980 km).

Weights: Max take-off, 22,750 lb (10 319 kg).

Accommodation: Flight crew of two and typical passenger seating for six to nine in choice of interior layouts.

Status: Prototype (with Garrett TFE731 engines) Learjet 60 (modification of original Model 55 prototype) flown on 18 October 1990 as a proof-of-concept vehicle. Re-engined with PW305s, this was scheduled to resume flight test in March 1991. Certification is expected to enable deliveries to commence in the fourth quarter of 1992.

Notes: The Model 60 is based upon the Model 55C, retaining the same wing, tail unit and 'Delta-Fins'. With an unchanged fuselage cross section, the Model 60 has a 43-in (109-cm) cabin stretch, improving passenger comfort and affording greater flexibility of interior design, approximately 28 in (71 cm) of this being added to the forward parallel section. The PW305 has been selected for its low specific fuel consumption, and the 'hot and high' performance of the Learjet 60 is demonstrated by its alleged ability to fly, for example, from Aspen, Colorado, on an ISA +20 degC day with four passengers and reach either coast.

LEARJET 60

Dimensions: Span, 43 ft 9 in (13,34 m); length, 58 ft 8 in (17,88 m); height, 14 ft 8 in (4,47 m); wing area, 264·5 sq ft (24,57 m²).

LET L 610

Country of Origin: Czechoslovakia.
Type: Short-haul regional transport.
Power Plant: Two 1,822 shp (1,358 kW) Motorlet M 602 or 1,870 shp (1,395 kW) General Electric CT7-9B turboprops.
Performance: (M 602) Max cruise speed, 304 mph (490 km/h) at 23,620 ft (7 200 m); range cruise, 253 mph (408 km/h) at 23,620 ft (7 200 m); max initial climb, 1,870 ft/min (9,5 m/sec); service ceiling, 35,270 ft (10 750 m); range with 45 min reserves, 540 mls (870 km) with max payload, 1,495 mls (2 406 km) with max fuel.
Weights: Operational empty, 19,841 lb (9 000 kg); max take-off, 30,865 lb (14 000 kg).
Accommodation: Crew of two and standard arrangement for 40 passengers four abreast. Alternative mixed passenger/cargo and all-cargo layouts available.
Status: First of three flying prototypes flown on 28 December 1988, with first two production aircraft having been scheduled for delivery to the Soviet Union early 1991 for pre-certification testing. Five L 610s to be delivered during 1991 with 10 following in 1992. Demonstration aircraft powered by CT7-9B engines expected to enter flight test September 1991, with production of similarly-powered aircraft expected to commence late 1992.
Notes: Designed primarily to meet a Soviet requirement for an aircraft to complement the 60-seat Il-114 regional airliner, the L 610 is expected to be supplied to the Soviet Union in substantial numbers from 1993. In order to increase the attractiveness of the aircraft on the western market, the L 610 is to be offered with the General Electric CT7-9B engine with which it is anticipated that the L 610 will obtain US certification in 1992. The L 610 has been designed for soft field operation and for descent rates demanded by 'difficult' strips.

LET L 610

Dimensions: Span, 84 ft 0 in (25,60 m); length, 70 ft 3¼ in (21,42 m); height, 24 ft 11½ in (7,61 m); wing area, 602·8 sq ft (56,00 m²).

LOCKHEED L-100-30 SUPER HERCULES

Country of Origin: USA.

Type: Medium- and long-haul cargo transport.

Power Plant: Four 4,508 shp (3 362 kW) Allison 501-D22A (T56-A-15) turboprops.

Performance: Max cruise speed (at 120,000 lb/54 430 kg), 355 mph (571 km/h) at 20,000 ft (6 100 m); max initial climb, 1,700 ft/min (8,64 m/sec); range (with 51,054-lb/23 158-kg payload and 45 min reserves), 1,536 mls (2 472 km), (zero payload and 45 min reserves), 5,562 mls (8 950 km).

Weights: Operational empty, 77,736 lb (35 260 kg); max take-off, 155, 000 lb (70 310 kg).

Accommodation: Normal flight crew of four and provision for a maximum payload of 51,054 lb (23 158 kg), loads including such heavy equipment as a 26,640-lb (12 080-kg) refuelling trailer or up to seven 463L freight pallets. One hundred and twenty-eight combat-equipped troops or 92 paratroops may be carried, and in the medevac role 97 casualty stretchers plus medical attendants may be carried.

Status: Some 1,970 Hercules had been delivered by the beginning of 1991, including about 120 commercial models, and production was continuing at two – three aircraft monthly.

Notes: The L-100-30 Super Hercules and its military equivalent, the C-130H-30, are stretched versions of the current basic Hercules, the C-130H. The original stretched commercial model, the L-100-20, embodied a 100-in (2,54-m) fuselage extension by comparison with the basic military version, and the L-100-30, intended for both commercial and military applications, has a further 80-in (2,03-m) fuselage stretch. The equivalent C-130H-30 serves with a dozen air forces, 30 RAF C-130H (C Mk 1) aircraft being modified to this standard (C Mk 3). The Hercules has been in continuous production for 37 years.

LOCKHEED L-100-30 SUPER HERCULES

Dimensions: Span, 132 ft 7 in (40,41 m); length, 112 ft 9 in (34,37 m); height, 38 ft 3 in (11,66 m); wing area, 1,745 sq ft (162,12 m²).

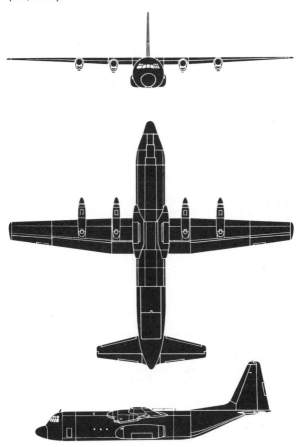

LOCKHEED F-117A

Country of Origin: USA.

Type: Single-seat low-altitude low-observable interdictor.

Power Plant: Two 10,800 lb st (48·0 kN) class General Electric F404-GE-F1D2 turbofans.

Performance: (Esimated) Max speed, 700 mph at sea level, or Mach = 0·92; normal max operating speed, 648 mph (1 043 km/h) at 5,000 ft (1 525 m), or Mach = 0·87; normal cruise, 460 mph (740 mph) at 30,000 ft (9 145 m).

Weights: (Approximate) Empty equipped, 30,000 lb (13 608 kg); max take-off, 52,500 lb (23 814 kg).

Armament: Up to 5,000 lb (2 270 kg) of ordnance accommodated by internal weapons bay, a typical load being two 2,000-lb (907-kg) laser-guided Mk 84 Paveway II bombs.

Status: First (pre-series) F-117A flown on 15 June 1981, with first customer (USAF) delivery mid 1982. Fifty-nine ordered and produced at a rate of eight annually, with last being delivered 12 July 1990.

Notes: A radical design affording low radar, infra-red and optical signatures, the F-117A is of unique, multi-faceted shape and possesses the primary role of defence suppression with internally-housed laser-guided bombs or missiles. Most aspects of the design were dictated by stealth considerations, and the F-117A is primarily of aluminium construction, both fuselage and wings being coated with several types of radar absorbent material. The entire fuselage surface consists of flat planes set in a limited number of alignments, the sharply swept (67 deg at leading edge) wing and the swept vee-type tail also being faceted. The F-117A achieved initial operational capability in October 1983 with the USAF's 4450th Tactical Group (redesignated 37th Tactical Fighter Wing in October 1989), but its existence was not officially acknowledged until November 1988.

Dimensions: Span, 43 ft 4 in (13,20 m); length, 65 ft 11 in (20,08 m); height, 12 ft 5 in (3,78 m).

LOCKHEED YF-22

Country of Origin: USA.

Type: Single-seat air superiority fighter.

Power Plant: Two 32,000–35,000 lb st (142–156 kN) category General Electric YF120-GE-100 or Pratt & Whitney YF119-PW-100 variable-cycle turbofans.

Performance: (Estimated) Max speed, 915 mph (1 470 km/h) at low altitude, or Mach = 1·2, 1,190 mph (1 915 km/h) above 36,000 ft (10 975 m), or Mach = 1·8; max sustained cruise, 925–990 mph (1 490–1 595 km/h) above 36,000 ft (10 975 m), or Mach = 1·4–1·5; combat radius (internal fuel and full AAM armament), 800–900 mls (1 290–1 450 km).

Weights: (Estimated) Empty, 33,000 lb (14 970 kg); normal loaded, 55,000 lb (24 950 kg).

Armament: One 20-mm M61 rotary cannon and two short-range AIM-9 AAMs in centre weapons bay of three in line abreast with two AIM-120 medium-range AAMs in each of the outboard bays.

Status: First of two YF-22 prototypes (with YF120 engines) flown on 29 September 1990, and second (with YF119 engines) following on 30 October. If selected to meet the USAF's ATF requirement, four F-22s are expected to be delivered in each of 1996 and 1997, with 12 following in 1998, 24 in 1999 and 36 in the year 2000 when it is anticipated that operational capability will be achieved. The US Navy will evaluate the chosen ATF with a view to a navalised version as a successor to the F-14.

Notes: Developed by Lockheed Aeronautical Systems teamed with General Dynamics and Boeing, the YF-22 was competing at the beginning of 1991 with the Northrop/McDonnell Douglas YF-23 (see pages 170–1) to fulfil the ATF (Advanced Tactical Fighter) requirement. Unlike its competitor, the YF-22 features two-dimensional thrust-vectoring engine nozzles to enhance manoeuvrability.

LOCKHEED YF-22

Dimensions: Span, 43 ft 0 in (13,10 m); length, 64 ft 2 in (19,56 m); height, 17 ft $8\frac{7}{8}$ in (5,40 m).

LOCKHEED P-3C ORION

Country of Origin: USA.

Type: Long-range maritime patrol aircraft.

Power Plant: Four 4,910 ehp (3,661 kW) Allison T56-A-14W turboprops.

Performance: Max speed (at 105,000 lb/47 625 kg), 473 mph (761 km/h) at 15,000 ft (4 570 m); econ cruise, 378 mph (608 km/h) at 25,000 ft (7 620 m); patrol speed, 237 mph (381 km/h) at 1,500 ft (457 m); max initial climb, 1,950 ft/min (9,9 m/sec); mission radius (three hours on station at 1,500 ft/ 457 m), 1,550 mls (2 494 km); max mission radius (no time on station at 135,000 lb/61 235 kg), 2,383 mls (3 835 km).

Weights: Empty, 61,491 lb (27 890 kg); normal loaded, 135.000 lb (61 235 kg); max take-off, 142,000 lb (64 410 kg).

Accommodation: Normal crew of 10 including five in tactical compartment.

Armament: Eight Mk 54 depth bombs, eight 560-lb (254-kg) Mk 82 or 980-lb (444,5-kg) Mk 83 bombs, eight Mk 46 or six Mk 50 torpedoes internally and externally. Max total weapons load includes six 2,000-lb (907-kg) mines underwing and 7,252-lb (3 290-kg) internal load can include two Mk 101 depth bombs and four Mk 44 torpedoes.

Status: The prototype Orion (YP-3C) flew on 8 October 1968, and orders for all versions (including the prototype) totalled 650 aircraft at the beginning of 1991. Of these, the 642nd (a CP-140A Arcturus version for Canada) is scheduled to roll off the line in May 1991, with deliveries being resumed in 1995 (with eight P-3Cs for South Korea).

Notes: The P-3 Orion serves with Australia, Canada, Iran, Japan, Netherlands, New Zealand, Norway, Pakistan, Portugal and Spain, in addition to the US. Licence manufacture is being undertaken in Japan by Kawasaki, 98 having been ordered by the beginning of 1991 (including three US-built aircraft).

LOCKHEED P-3C ORION

Dimensions: Span, 99 ft 8 in (30,37 m); length, 116 ft 10 in (35,61 m); height, 33 ft 8½ in (10,29 m); wing area, 1,300 sq ft (120,77 m²).

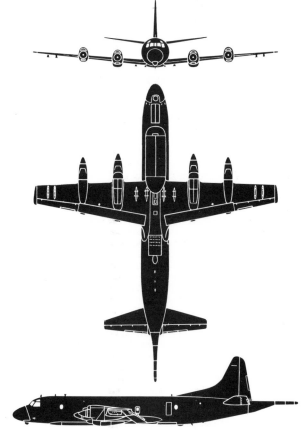

McDONNELL DOUGLAS C-17A

Country of Origin: USA.
Type: Heavy lift military freighter.
Power Plant: Four 41,700 lb st (185·5 kN) Pratt & Whitney F117-PW-100 turbofans.
Performance: (Manufacturer's estimates) Max cruise, 508 mph (818 km/h) at 36,000 ft (10 975 m), 403 mph (648 km/h) at low altitude; range (unrefuelled), 3,225 mls (5 190 km) with 129,200-lb (58 605-kg) payload, 3,110 mls (5 000 km) with 158,500-lb (71 895-kg) payload, 2,765 mls (4 445 km) with 167,000-lb (75 750-kg) payload.
Weights: (Projected) Operational empty, 269,000 lb (122 016 kg); max take-off, 580,000 lb (263 083 kg).
Accommodation: Normal flight crew of two plus a loadmaster. Main cargo hold able to accept three AH-64A helicopters or Army wheeled vehicles, including five-ton expandable vans in two side-by-side rows. Airdrop capability includes up to 102 paratroops, single platforms of up to 60,000 lb (27 215 kg), or multiple platforms of up to 110,000 lb (49 895 kg).
Status: Development aircraft scheduled to enter flight test in June 1991. Two additional aircraft to be used in the flight development programme, and planning at the beginning of 1991 envisaged production of 120 C-17As for the USAF, with initial operational capability being achieved in 1993.
Notes: Intended to provide inter-theatre and theatre airlift of outsize loads, including armoured vehicles, directly into airfields in potential conflict areas, the C-17A will be able to offer a short-field performance, operating from 3,000-ft (915-m) runways. The USAF originally planned to acquire 210 C-17As, but cutbacks in procurement during 1990 dramatically reduced this number.

McDONNELL DOUGLAS C-17A

Dimensions: Span, 165 ft 0 in (50,29 m); length, 174 ft 0 in (53,04 m); height, 55 ft 1 in (16,79 m); wing area, 3,800 sq ft (353 m²).

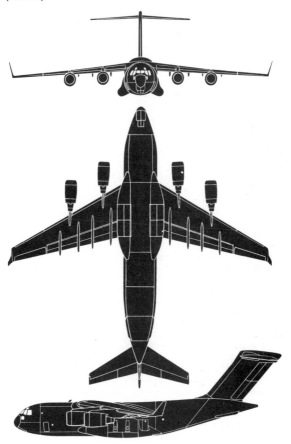

McDONNELL DOUGLAS F-15E EAGLE

Country of Origin: USA.

Type: Two-seat dual-role (air-air and air-ground) fighter.

Power Plant: Two 14,370 lb st (63·9 kN) dry and 23,450 lb st (104·3 kN) reheat Pratt & Whitney F100-PW-220 turbofans.

Performance: Max speed (short-endurance dash), 1,676 mph (2 698 km/h) at 40,000 ft (12 190 m), or Mach = 2·54, (sustained), 1,518 mph (2 443 km/h), or Mach = 2·3; max combat radius, 790 mls (1 270 km); max range (with conformal tanks and max external fuel), 2,765 mls (4 445 km).

Weights: Basic operational empty, 31,700 lb (14 379 kg); max take-off, 81,000 lb (36 741 kg).

Armament: One 20-mm six-barrel rotary cannon and max ordnance load of 24,500 lb (11 113 kg) on centreline and two wing stations plus four tangential carriers on conformal fuel tanks. For air-air mission up to four each AIM-7 and AIM-9 AAMs or up to eight AIM-120 AAMs.

Status: First production F-15E flown on 11 December 1986, with the last of 200 aircraft for the USAF to be completed in June 1993.

Notes: The F-15E is derived from the basic F-15 for long-range, deep interdiction air-ground missions by day or night, and some 60 per cent of the structure has been redesigned. The first F-15E to be powered by F100-PW-229 engines affording 29,000 lb st (129 kN) with afterburning flew on 2 May 1990, and these engines will be installed in all new production F-15Es from August 1991. A proposed single-seat air superiority version of the F-15E intended for export is the F-15F. This retains the AN/APG-70 radar, but lacks air-to-ground modes, and has no provision for conformal fuel tanks. During 1990, the USAF was studying minimally modified F-15X and more extensively reconfigured F-15XX proposals as possible fall-backs for the ATF (Advanced Tactical Fighter).

McDONNELL DOUGLAS F-15E EAGLE

Dimensions: Span, 42 ft 9¾ in (13,05 m); length, 63 ft 9in (19,43 m); height, 18 ft 5½ in (5,63 m); wing area, 608 sq ft (56,50 m²).

McDONNELL DOUGLAS F/A-18 HORNET

Country of Origin: USA.

Type: Single-seat shipboard and shore-based multi-role fighter and two-seat trainer and attack aircraft.

Power Plant: Two 19,600 lb st (47·15 kN) dry and 15,800 lb st (70·27 kN) reheat General Electric F404-GE-400 or 17,700 lb st (79 kN) reheat F404-GE-402 turbofans.

Performance: (F/A-18C with -400 engines) Max speed (AAMs on wingtip and fuselage stations), 1,190 mph (1 915 km/h) at 40,000 ft (12 150 m), or Mach = 1·8; max initial climb (half fuel and wingtip AAMs), 60,000 ft/min (304,6 m/sec); combat radius (air-to-air), 480 mls (770 km), (with three 315 US gal/1 192 l external tanks), 735 mls (1 180 km).

Weights: (F/A-18C) Empty, 23,050 lb (10 455 kg); loaded (fighter mission), 36,710 lb (16 651 kg), (attack), 49,224 lb (22 238 kg); max take-off, 56,000 lb (25 400 kg).

Armament: One 20-mm rotary cannon and up to 17,000 lb (7 711 kg) of ordnance/fuel distributed between nine stations.

Status: First of 11 development aircraft flown on 18 November 1978, with first production F/A-18A following in April 1980. Deliveries of 410 F/A-18As (and two-seat F/A-18Bs) completed 1987 when supplanted by F/A-18C (and two-seat F/A-18D). Some 690 Hornets (all versions) delivered to US Navy and Marine Corps by beginning of 1991.

Notes: All F/A-18Cs and Ds delivered from November 1989 have all-weather and night attack capability, the F/A-18D two-seater (illustrated above) supplanting the A-6 Intruder in US Marine Corps service in the attack role from late 1989. Exports have comprised Canada (98 single-seaters and 40 two-seaters), Spain (60 and 12), and Australia (57 and 18), all but two of the last being licence-built by ASTA. At the beginning of 1991, work was proceeding on a Kuwaiti contract for Hornets (32 and 8), a South Korean contract for 120 aircraft (all but 12 to be indigenously assembled or co-produced) was under negotiation and a Swiss contract was in abeyance.

McDONNELL DOUGLAS F/A-18 HORNET

Dimensions: Span, 37 ft 6 in (11,43 m); length, 56 ft 0 in (17,07 m); height, 15 ft 4 in (4,67 m); wing area, 400 sq ft (37,16 m²).

McDONNELL DOUGLAS MD-11

Country of Origin: USA.

Type: Long-haul commercial transport.

Power Plant: Three 61,500 lb st (273·6 kN) General Electric CF6-80C2-D1F, 60,000 lb st (266·9 kN) Pratt & Whitney PW4460 or 65,000 lb st (289·1 kN) Rolls-Royce Trent 665 turbofans.

Performance: (PW4460 engines) Max speed, 597 mph (962 km/h) at 27,000 ft (8 230 m), or Mach=0·87; max cruise, 579 mph (932 km/h) at 30,000 ft (9 150 m); econ cruise, 544 mph (876 km/h) at 35,000 ft (10 670 m); max initial climb, 2,770 ft/min (14,07 m/sec); service ceiling, 32,600 ft (9 935 m); range (max payload with FAR international reserves), 5,760 mls (9 270 km).

Weights: Operational empty, 277,500 lb (125 874 kg); max take-off, 602,500 lb (273 289 kg).

Accommodation: Crew of two and max seating for 405 passengers 10 abreast, with a typical two-class arrangement for 323 passengers.

Status: First and second of five MD-11s being used for flight test (and later to be refurbished for customer delivery) flew on 10 January and 1 March 1990 with CF6 engines, and third, with PW4460 engines followed on 26 April. Certification of the CF6-engined version achieved on 8 November 1990, with first customer delivery (to Finnair) taking place on 29 November. At the beginning of 1991, 178 firm orders (plus 197 other commitments) had been recorded.

Notes: Three versions of the MD-11 are available: that described above, the Combi mixed passenger/cargo aircraft and the all-freight MD-11F. A stretched version of the MD-11 was being offered at the beginning of 1991 as the MD-12 with a 34·1-ft (10,4-m) fuselage stretch and a max weight of 669,090 lb (303 500 kg). A second version of the MD-12 will have a completely new wing.

McDONNELL DOUGLAS MD-11

Dimensions: Span, 169 ft 6 in (51,66 m); length, 200 ft 10 in (61,21 m); height, 57 ft 9 in (17,60 m); wing area, 3,648 sq ft (338,90 m²).

McDONNELL DOUGLAS MD-87

Country of Origin: USA.
Type: Short- to medium-haul commercial transport.
Power Plant: Two 20,000 lb st (88·9 kN) Pratt & Whitney JT8D-217C turbofans.
Performance: Max cruise speed, 575 mph (925 km/h) at 27,000 ft (8 230 m); econ cruise, 522 mph (840 km/h) at 33,000 ft (10 060 m); range cruise, 505 mph (813 km/h) at 35,000 ft (10 670 m); range (with 130 passengers and standard fuel), 2,731 mls (4 395 km), (optional fuel), 3,260 mls (5 243 km).
Weights: Operational empty (standard), 73,157 lb (33 183 kg), (optional), 74,629 lb (33 851 kg); max take-off (standard), 140,000 lb (63 503 kg), (optional), 149,500 lb (67 812 kg).
Accommodation: Flight crew of two and maximum optional passenger seating capacity for 139 five abreast with optional mixed class arrangements.
Status: First MD-87 flown on 4 December 1986, with first customer deliveries (to Austrian and Finnair) following in October 1987. Total of 100 ordered by beginning of 1991 (within overall total of some 1,150 orders for MD-80 variants) with some 30 delivered. Production rate at beginning of 1991 (all MD-80 models) was reducing from 3·0 to 2·5 aircraft weekly.
Notes: The MD-80 series was evolved from the DC-9 and is currently offered in five versions, the MD-81, -82, -83 and -88 having a common fuselage length of 135 ft 6 in (41,30 m) and an overall length of 147 ft 10 in (45,06 m), and the MD-87 (described and illustrated) having a shorter fuselage. A JT8D-290-powered 105-seat version of the MD-87 was being proposed at the beginning of 1991. All versions have fundamentally the same wing, but differ in weight and power plant. The MD-90, scheduled to fly early 1993, represents a further stage in the incremental development of the basic design powered by International Aero Engines V2500 turbofans.

McDONNELL DOUGLAS MD-87

Dimensions: Span, 107 ft 10 in (32,85 m); length, 130 ft 5 in (39,75 m); height, 30 ft 6 in (9,30 m); wing area, 1,270 sq ft (117,98 m²).

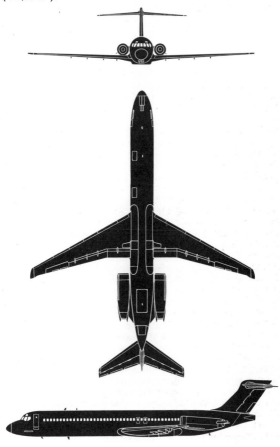

McDONNELL DOUGLAS/BRITISH AEROSPACE T-45A GOSHAWK

Country of Origin: USA (United Kingdom).

Type: Tandem two-seat carrier-capable basic/advanced trainer.

Power Plant: One 5,840 lb st (25·98 kN) Rolls-Royce/Turboméca F405-RR-401 (Adour Mk 871) turbofan.

Performance: (Estimated at 12,758 lb/5 787 kg) Max speed, 620 mph (997 km/h) at 8,000 ft (2 440 m), 573 mph (922 km/h) at 30,000 ft (9 150 m); max initial climb, 6,982 ft/min (35,47 m/sec); time to 30,000 ft (9 150 m), 7·2 min; ferry range (internal fuel only), 1,150 mls (1 850 km).

Weights: (Estimated) Empty, 9,399 lb (4 263 kg); max take-off, 12,758 lb (5 787 kg).

Status: The first of two full-scale engineering development T-45As was flown on 16 April 1988, with US Navy requirement for total of 302 aircraft. At the beginning of 1991, it was anticipated that initial production would comprise 48 aircraft with deliveries commencing during the course of January 1992.

Notes: The T-45A Goshawk has been derived from the British Aerospace Hawk as part of an integrated training system (T-45TS) embodying aircraft, academics, simulators and logistics support. Seventy-six per cent of the manufacture of the T-45A is being undertaken in the USA, but a substantial programme delay has resulted from problems experienced during initial flight testing which included longitudinal control system instability, abrupt pitch change resulting from speed brake deployment, excessive yaw and Dutch roll. Modifications have included an uprated engine, full leading-edge slats, redesigned speed brakes and introduction of a ventral fin. About 60 per cent of the internal structure now differs from that of the Hawk. Initial operational capability is now likely to be attained during the course of 1992, some two years late.

McDONNELL DOUGLAS/BRITISH AEROSPACE T-45A GOSHAWK

Dimensions: Span, 30 ft 9¾ in (9,39 m); length (including probe), 39 ft 3⅛ in (11,97 m); height, 13 ft 5 in (4,09 m); wing area, 179·64 sq ft (16,69 m²).

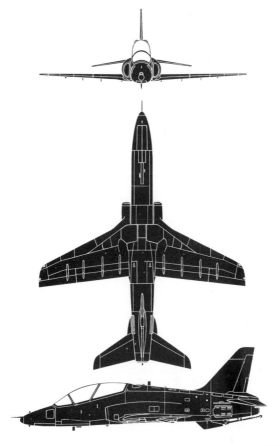

McDONNELL DOUGLAS TAV-8B HARRIER II

Countries of Origin: USA and United Kingdom.
Type: Tandem two-seat conversion trainer.
Power Plant: One 21,450 lb st (95·42 kN) Rolls-Royce F402-RR-406 (Pegasus 11-21) vectored-thrust turbofan.
Performance: Max speed, 667 mph (1 074 km/h) at sea level, or Mach=0·87, 587 mph (945 km/h) at 36,000 ft (10 975 m), or Mach=0·9; ferry range (with two 300 US gal/1 136 l external tanks retained), 1,647 mls (2 650 km).
Weights: Operational empty (including crew), 14,223 lb (6 451 kg); max take-off (for STO), 29,750 lb (13 495 kg).
Armament: (Weapons training) Two underwing stores stations which can carry up to six Mk 76 practice bombs, two LAU-68 rocket launchers or other weapons.
Status: First TAV-8B flown on 21 October 1986, with initial deliveries to the US Marine Corps commencing in August 1987. Twenty-three of planned 27-aircraft procurement delivered to the service by the beginning of 1991, when two were to be acquired by each of the Italian and Spanish navies. Fourteen essentially similar aircraft ordered for the RAF in February 1990 as Harrier T Mk 10s.
Notes: A two-seat derivative of the AV-8B single-seat close support aircraft, which also serves with the Spanish Navy as the EAV-8B (Matador II), is to be acquired by the Italian Navy and is operated by the RAF as the Harrier GR Mks 5 and 7 (see pages 62–63), the TAV-8B has been developed by McDonnell Douglas with British Aerospace as sub-contractor. It features a new two-seat forward fuselage and a new vertical tail, but is in other respects similar to the single-seater. The RAF's Harrier T Mk 10 version (illustrated on the opposite page) will be equipped with forward-looking infrared and night vision systems similar to those of the GR Mk 7, and will be delivered from early 1994.

McDONNELL DOUGLAS TAV-8B HARRIER II

Dimensions: Span, 30 ft 4 in (9,24 m); length, 50 ft 3 in (15,32 m); height, 13 ft $4\frac{3}{4}$ in (4,08 m); wing area (including LERX), 238·7 sq ft (22,18 m^2).

MIKOYAN MIG-29 (FULCRUM)

Country of Origin: USSR.

Type: Single-seat counterair fighter.

Power Plant: Two 11,243 lb st (50·0 kN) dry and 18,300 lb st (81·39 kN) Leningrad (Klimov) RD-33 augmented bypass turbojet.

Performance: Max speed (four R-27 and two R-73 AAMs), 1,518 mph (2 445 km/h) at 36,100 ft (11 000 m), or Mach = 2·3, 805 mph (1 300 km/h) at sea level, or Mach = 1·06; max initial climb, 64,960 ft/min (330 m/sec); service ceiling, 55,775 ft (17 000 m); combat radius (subsonic area intercept with 330 Imp gal/1 500 l centreline tank and four R-27 AAMs), 630 mls (1 015 km); ferry range, 1,800 mls (2 900 km).

Weights: Approx operational empty, 18,025 lb (8 175 kg); normal loaded, 33,598 lb (15 240 kg); max take-off, 40,785 lb (18 500 kg).

Armament: One 30-mm GSh-301 cannon and two medium-range R-27 *Alamo-A* radar-homing plus six close-range R-60 *Aphid* AAMs.

Status: First prototype flown 6 October 1977, with initial production deliveries late 1983 and initial operational capability achieved (with SovAF) early 1985. Some 600 delivered to SovAF by beginning of 1991 when 250 had been ordered by or delivered to foreign customers.

Notes: The MiG-29, in its *Fulcrum-A* form (illustrated above) is in service with 12 countries, together with the *Fulcrum-B* (MiG-29UB) two-seat combat trainer. The *Fulcrum-C* (illustrated opposite) features a raised dorsal fairing accommodating equipment transferred from the lower fuselage to provide for additional fuel. The *Fulcrum-D* (MiG-29K) is a navalised version tested 1989–90 aboard the carrier *Kuznetsov* (formerly *Tbilisi*).

MIKOYAN MIG-29 (FULCRUM)

Dimensions: Span, 37 ft 4½ in (11,36 m); length (including probe), 56 ft 9⅞ in (17,32 m); height, 15 ft 6¼ in (4,73 m); wing area, 409·04 sq ft (38,00 m²).

MIKOYAN MIG-31 (FOXHOUND)

Country of Origin: USSR.

Type: Tandem two-seat all-weather interceptor fighter.

Power Plant: Two 33,070+ lb st (147·1 kN) reheat MKB (Soloviev) D-30F-6 turbofans.

Performance: Max speed, 1,520 mph (2 445 km/h) at 36,100 ft (11 000 m), or Mach=2·3; combat radius (area intercept with four long-range and four close-combat AAMs), 447 mls (720 km), (with two drop tanks on outer underwing pylons), 870 mls (1 400 km); approx service ceiling, 78,740 ft (24 000 m).

Weights: (Estimated) Empty equipped, 47,000 lb (21 320 kg); normal loaded, 65,000–70,000 lb (29 485–31 750 kg); max take-off, 99,205 lb (45 000 kg).

Armament: One 23-mm or 30-mm cannon in starboard side of lower fuselage and eight (four in tandem pairs on fuselage centreline and two on each of two wing pylons) AA-9 Amos semi-active, radar-homing long-range AAMs, or four AA-9 Amos and four AA-8 Aphid (R-60) close-combat IR-homing AAMs.

Status: First flown in September 1975, the MiG-31 was first deployed by the *Voyska PVO* air defence forces from early 1983. Some 170–180 were reportedly in service at the beginning of 1991, when production was continuing at Gorkiy.

Notes: The MiG-31 possesses a lookdown/shootdown pulse-Doppler weapons system, its multiple-target engagement capability enabling it to track 10 targets and engage four targets above and below the aircraft simultaneously. Fundamentally based on the 'sixties technology MiG-25, which it closely resembles externally, the MiG-31 is, nevertheless, of largely new design. An unusual feature is the staggered tandem arrangement of the mainwheels which spread the aircraft weight during take-off and landing.

MIKOYAN MIG-31 (FOXHOUND)

Dimensions: (Estimated) Span, 45 ft 9 in (13,94 m); length (excluding probe), 68 ft 10 in (21,00 m); height, 18 ft 6 in (5,63 m); wing area, 602·8 sq ft (56,00 m²).

MYASISHCHEV M-17 (MYSTIC)

Country of Origin: USSR.

Type: Single-seat high-altitude reconnaissance and research aircraft.

Power Plant: (Stratospherica) One 15,430 lb st (68·64 kN) RKBM (Koliesov) RD-36-51V turbojet, or (Geophysica) two 11,025 lb st (49 kN) MKB (Soloviev) turbofans.

Performance: (Stratospherica) Max speed, 466 mph (750 km/h) at 29,530 ft (9 000 m); max continuous cruise, 404 mph (650 km/h); time to altitude (with 4,410-lb/2 000-kg payload), 4·7 min to 19,685 ft (6 000 m), 8·73 min to 39,370 ft (12 000 m), 25·08 min to 65,615 ft (20 000 m); max endurance, 6·5 hrs at 55,775 ft.

Weights: (Stratospherica) Max take-off, 44,092 lb (20 000 kg).

Status: The M-17 (in its Stratospherica version) was first reported at the Ramenskoye flight test centre in 1982 when it was assigned the provisional reporting designation of Ram-M in the West. Only two prototypes of the initial version are believed to have been built and flown, an improved development referred to as the Geophysica entering flight test in 1988.

Notes: The M-17, assigned the Western reporting name of Mystic, was apparently intended as a counterpart of the USAF's Lockheed TR-1 high-altitude strategic reconnaissance aircraft. It may be presumed that changes in operational requirements coupled with the development of a superior twin-engined version of the basic design (Geophysica) led to discontinuation of development of the single-engined model (Stratospherica) which was subsequently described by the Soviet media as a civil research aircraft, its tasks including that of a flying laboratory to monitor the ozone layer. The Stratospherica version of the M-17 established 25 world records in March, April and May 1990 for speed and altitude in the FAI class C-1 Group III sub-class C-1-i. The twin-engined Geophysica version (illustrated above and opposite) differs primarily in having an elongated fuselage and raised pilot position.

MYASISHCHEV M-17 (MYSTIC)

Dimensions: Span, 123 ft 0½ in (37,50 m); length, 74 ft 5¾ in (22,70 m); height, 15 ft 9 in (4,80 m).

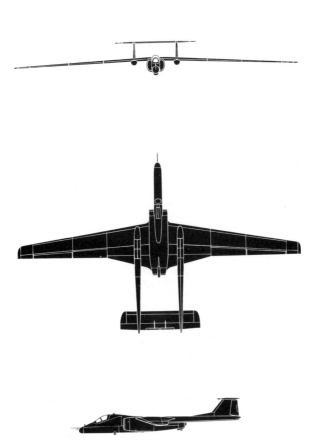

NAMC K-8

Country of Origin: China.

Type: Tandem two-seat basic trainer and light ground attack aircraft.

Power Plant: One 3,600 lb st (16·0 kN) Garrett TFE731-2A-2A turbofan.

Performance: (Manufacturer's estimates) Max speed, 503 mph (810 km/h) at sea level; max initial climb, 5,905 ft/min (30 m/sec); service ceiling, 42,650 ft (13 000 m); endurance, 3·0 hrs; max range, 1,430 mls (2 300 km).

Weights: Empty equipped, 5,637 lb (2 557 kg); loaded (clean), 7,716 lb (3 500 kg); max take-off, 9,259 lb (4 200 kg).

Armament: (Attack) One 23-mm cannon pod under fuselage centreline and four wing stores stations capable of carrying bombs, gun or rocket pods or missiles.

Status: The first of five prototypes (three flying and two static test) was flown on 21 November 1990, and the Pakistan Air Force has contracted to procure the first 25 series aircraft with deliveries commencing late 1992.

Notes: The K-8, developed almost independently by NAMC (Nanchang Aircraft Manufacturing Company), has evolved in collaboration with the Pakistan Aeronautical Complex which contributed maintenance and operational expertise. Current planning calls for the initial production batch to be supplied to the Pakistan Air Force, partially-equipped airframes being delivered by NAMC and completion being undertaken at Kamra by the Pakistan Aeronautical Complex. Service entry is expected to take place mid 1993. No order had been placed on behalf of the People's Republic of China Air Force at the time of closing for press, but the K-8 is to be evaluated by that service and may possibly be adopted with the ZMKB/ZVL DV-2 engine which it is proposed be licence-manufactured in China.

NAMC K-8

Dimensions: Span, 31 ft 7¼ in (9,63 m); length (including probe), 38 ft 0¾ in (11,60 m); height, 13 ft 9¾ in (4,21 m); wing area, 183·5 sq ft (17,05 m²).

NORTHROP B-2A

Country of Origin: USA.

Type: Low-observable strategic bomber.

Power Plant: Four 19,000 lb st (84·5 kN) General Electric F118-GE-110 turbofans.

Performance: Max speed (estimated), 595–628 mph (955–1 010 km/h) at 50,000 ft, or Mach = 0·9–0·95; range (with eight SRAMS and eight B83 bombs), 7,255 mls (11 675 km) HI-HI-HI, 5,067 mls (8 154 km) HI-LO-HI, 1,152 mls (1 853 km) at low altitude).

Weights: Empty, 100,000–110,000 lb (45 360–49 900 kg); max take-off, 371,330 lb (168 433 kg).

Armament: Rotary launcher in each of two side-by-side weapons bay for maximum of 16 SRAMs (Short-Range Attack Missiles). Alternative weapons include B61 and B63 free-fall nuclear bombs, 1,000-lb (453,6-kg) Mk 36 sea mines and 500-lb (227-kg) Mk 82 or 750-lb (340-kg) M117 bombs. Max weapon load, 50,000 lb (22 680 kg).

Status: The first B-2A was flown on 17 July 1989 and the second on 19 October 1990. Four more full scale development aircraft expected to join the flight test programme during the course of 1991. All but one to be refurbished for delivery to USAF Strategic Air Command. Original USAF requirement for 133 B-2As, but at the time of closing for press it appeared likely that procurement would total 75 aircraft.

Notes: Possessing a crew of two, the B-2A advanced-technology bomber has low observable characteristics and is largely of composite construction, some structures being laminates of composites and metals.

NORTHROP B-2A

Dimensions: Span, 172 ft 0 in (52,43 m); length, 69 ft 0 in (21,03 m); height, 17 ft 0 in (5,18 m).

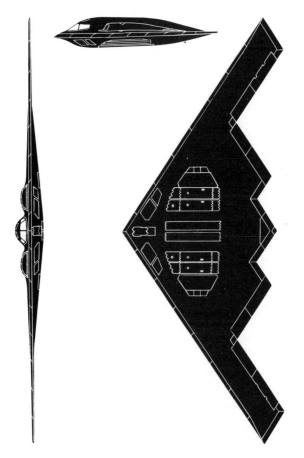

NORTHROP/McDONNELL DOUGLAS YF-23

Country of Origin: USA.

Type: Single-seat air superiority fighter.

Power Plant: Two 32,000–35,000 lb st (142–156 kN) category Pratt & Whitney YF119-PW-100 or General Electric YF120-GE-100 variable-cycle turbofans.

Performance: (Estimated) Max speed, 915 mph (1 470 km/h) at low altitude, or Mach = 1·2, 1,190 mph (1 915 km/h) above 36,000 ft (10 975 m), or Mach = 1·8; max sustained cruise, 925–990 mph (1 490–1 595 km/h) above 36,000 ft (10 975 m), or Mach = 1·4–1·5; combat radius (internal fuel and full AAM armament), 800–900 mls (1 290–1 450 km).

Weights: (Estimated) Empty, 33,000 lb (14 970 kg); normal loaded, 55,000 lb (24 950 kg).

Armament: One 20-mm M61 rotary cannon and two short-range AIM-9 AAMs in forward of tandem weapons bays and four AIM-120 medium-range AAMs in vertically and horizontally staggered pairs in larger rear bay.

Status: First of two YF-23 prototypes (with YF119 engines) flown on 27 August 1990, and second (with YF120 engines) following on 26 October. If selected to fulfil USAF's ATF requirement, four F-23s will be produced in each of 1996 and 1997, 12 in 1998, 24 in 1999 and 36 in 2000, the year in which operational capability is to be achieved. The USAF has stated a requirement for 750 aircraft, but this is likely to be reduced.

Notes: At the beginning of 1991, the YF-23 was competing with the Lockheed YF-22 (see pages 142–3) to fulfil the ATF (Advanced Tactical Fighter) requirement. Technically innovative, with a 'trapezoidal' wing, the leading edges of which are swept back 40 deg and the trailing edges swept forward 40 deg, the YF-23 possesses low observable characteristics.

NORTHROP/McDONNELL DOUGLAS YF-23

Dimensions: Span, 43 ft 7¼ in (13,29 m); length, 67 ft 4¾ in (20,54 m); height, 13 ft 10¾ in (4,24 m).

PANAVIA TORNADO F MK 3

Country of Origin: United Kingdom.
Type: Tandem two-seat air defence fighter.
Power Plant: Two 9,100 lb st (40·5 kN) dry and 16,520 lb st (73·5 kN) Turbo-Union RB199-34R Mk 104 turbofans.
Performance: Max speed, 920 mph (1 480 km/h) at sea level, or Mach = 1·2, 1,450 mph (2 333 km/h) at 40,000 ft (12 190 m); time to 30,000 ft (9 145 m), 1·7 min; tactical radius (combat air patrol with two 330 Imp gal/1 500 l drop tanks and 2-hr loiter allowance), 350–450 mls (560–725 km); ferry range (with four 330 Imp gal/1 500 l external tanks), 2,650 mls (4 265 km).
Weights: Approx operational empty, 31,970 lb (14 500 kg); max take-off, 61,700 lb (27 986 kg).
Armament: One 27-mm cannon and four Sky Flash medium-range and four AIM-9L Sidewinder short-range AAMs.
Status: First of three F Mk 2 prototypes flown on 27 October 1979 followed by first of 18 production F Mk 2s (including six F Mk 2Ts) on 5 March 1984. Production subsequently switched to F Mk 3 of which deliveries commenced in July 1986 after initial flight on 20 November 1985. Orders for the RAF (including F Mk 2s) comprised 165 aircraft, and 24 similar aircraft (including six with dual controls) have been ordered by the Royal Saudi Air Force. Production of the Tornado (all versions) expected to be completed at end of 1992.
Notes: The definitive air defence version (ADV) for the RAF of the multi-national (UK, Federal Germany and Italy) interdictor strike (IDS) aircraft, the Tornado F Mk 3 equipped five operational RAF squadrons at the beginning of 1991, with a sixth forming. An electronic combat and reconnaissance (ECR) version of the basic IDS aircraft was in process of delivery to the *Luftwaffe* at the beginning of 1991.

PANAVIA TORNADO F MK 3

Dimensions: Span (25 deg sweep), 45 ft 7¼ in (13,90 m), (68 deg sweep), 28 ft 2½ in (8,59 m); length, 59 ft 3⅞ in (18,08 m); height, 18 ft 8½ in (5,70 m); wing area, 286·3 sq ft (26,60 m²).

PIAGGIO P.180 AVANTI

Country of Origin: Italy.

Type: Light corporate transport.

Power Plant: Two 850 shp/634 kW (flat rated from 1,485 shp/ 1,107 kW) Pratt & Whitney PT6A-66 turboprops.

Performance: Max speed, 460 mph (740 km/h) at 28,000 ft (8 535 m); max continuous cruise, 400 mph (644 km/h) at 39,000 ft (11 885 m); max initial climb, 3,100 ft/min (15,75 m/ sec); service ceiling, 41,000 ft (12 495 m); range (IFR reserves), 1,727 mls (2 780 km), VFR reserves, 2,095 mls (3 372 km).

Weights: Empty equipped, 7,200 lb (3 266 kg); max take-off, 10,900 lb (4 944 kg).

Accommodation: Pilot and co-pilot/passenger on flight deck with seating in main cabin for up to nine passengers. Standard configuration for seven passengers in individual seats.

Status: Two prototypes flown on 23 September 1986 and 15 May 1987, with first production aircraft flying on 29 January 1990. Full FAA certification obtained on 1 October 1990. Four series Avantis had been delivered by the beginning of 1991 in which year 14–16 are scheduled to be produced. A second assembly line (Duncan-Piaggio at Lincoln, Nebraska) will commence deliveries in 1992.

Notes: The Avanti is configurationally innovative in having a foreplane balancing an aft-located mainplane, a tailplane being retained for pitch control.

174

PIAGGIO P.180 AVANTI

Dimensions: Span, 46 ft 0½ in (14,03 m); length, 47 ft 3½ in (14,41 m); height, 12 ft 11 in (3,94 m); wing area, 172·22 sq ft (16,00 m²).

PILATUS PC-9

Country of Origin: Switzerland.

Type: Tandem two-seat basic/advanced trainer and target tug.

Power Plant: One 1,150 shp (857 kW) Pratt & Whitney Canada PT6A-62 turboprop flat-rated at 950 shp (708 kW).

Performance: (At 4,960 lb/2 250 kg) Max speed, 311 mph (500 km/h) at sea level, 345 mph (556 km/h) at 20,000 ft (6 100 m); max initial climb rate, 4,090 ft/min (20,8 m/sec); max range (five per cent fuel reserve plus 20 min), 1,020 mls (1 642 km) at 25,000 ft (7 620 m).

Weights: Basic empty, 3,715 lb (1 685 kg); max take-off (aerobatic), 4,960 lb (2 250 kg), (utility), 7,055 lb (3 200 kg).

Status: First and second prototypes flown on 7 May and 20 July 1984, with first production deliveries commencing late 1985, and 151 ordered by beginning of 1991. Customers comprise Angola (4), Australia (67), Burma (4), Cyprus (2), Iraq (20), Mexico (10), Saudi Arabia (30), Switzerland (4) and Germany (10). Of those supplied to Australia, two were delivered flyaway, six as kits and 11 as major components for assembly by Hawker de Havilland and ASTA; which companies are licence-manufacturing a further 48 with programme completion scheduled spring 1992.

Notes: Australian-built aircraft (PC-9As) have EFIS and low-pressure tyres as standard and those delivered to Germany (PC-9Bs) are operated by a private company on behalf of the *Luftwaffe* as target tugs. The four supplied to the Swiss *Flugwaffe* (against an eventual requirement for 12–16 aircraft) fulfil target-towing and target presentation tasks, and the service is considering the PC-9 for a 1993 requirement for a low-level tactics trainer. Saudi PC-9s have cockpit instrumentation compatible with that of the BAe Hawk.

PILATUS PC-9

Dimensions: Span, 33 ft 2½ in (10,12 m); length, 33 ft 4¾ in (10,17 m); height, 10 ft 8⅓ in (3,26 m); wing area, 175·3 sq ft (16,29 m²).

PILATUS PC-12

Country of Origin: Switzerland.

Type: Light utility and business transport.

Power Plant: One 1,200 shp (895 kW) Pratt & Whitney Canada PT6A-67B turboprop (flat rated from 1,780 shp (1,327 kW)).

Performance: (Manufacturer's estimates) Max cruise speed, 309 mph (497 km/h) at 25,000 ft (7 620 m); max initial climb, 2,050 ft/min (10,40 m/sec); max operating altitude, 25,000 ft (7 620 m); max range (45 min reserves), 1,843 mls (2 966 km).

Weights: Empty (freighter), 4,813 lb (2 183 kg), (passenger configuration), 5,260 lb (2 386 kg); max take-off, 8,818 lb (4 000 kg).

Accommodation: Pilot and co-pilot/passenger on flight deck and up to nine passengers in individual seats for commuter role, or six seats in executive version.

Status: First of two prototypes scheduled to enter flight test on 31 May 1991, with certification planned for mid 1992 and first customer deliveries in January 1993.

Notes: The PC-12, first announced in October 1989, is a pressurised multi-role transport, the multiple mission capabilities ranging from executive level transportation to long-distance delivery of freight and oversized equipment. Variants on offer include the PC-12 Combi which, able to carry four passengers in the main cabin, offers 210 cu ft (5,95 m³) of space for freight, the pure freighter version having 330 cu ft (9,34 m³) of cargo space available, a large cargo door being standard.

PILATUS PC-12

Dimensions: Span, 48 ft 3 in (13,78 m); length, 45 ft 10 in (13,96 m); height, 13 ft 7 in (4,14 m).

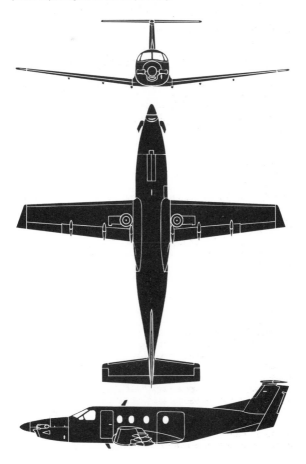

PZL-130TM TURBO ORLIK

Country of Origin: Poland.

Type: Tandem two-seat basic and multi-purpose trainer.

Power Plant: One 751 shp (560 kW) Walter M 601E or 550 shp (410 kW) Pratt & Whitney Canada PT6A-25A turboprop.

Performance: (M 601E) Max speed, 315 mph (507 km/h); max cruise, 273 mph (440 km/h) at sea level, 309 mph (498 km/h) at 15,000 ft (4 570 m); max initial climb, 3,190 ft/min (16,2 m/sec); service ceiling, 32,810 ft (10 000 m); max range (internal fuel), 652 mls (1 050 km) at 10,000 ft (3 050 m).

Weights: (M 601E) Empty equipped, 2,976 lb (1 350 kg); max take-off (aerobatic), 3,307 lb (1 500 kg), (with external stores), 4,358 lb (1 977 kg).

Status: The first Turbo Orlik (conversion of third piston-engined PZL-130 Orlik) was flown on 13 July 1986 with a PT6A engine, and the second flew on 12 January 1989 with an M 601E engine. Three Turbo Orliks included in batch of seven pre-series PZL-130s. No decision concerning series production had been announced by the beginning of 1991.

Notes: Derived from the piston-engined PZL-130 Orlik (Eaglet) for which see 1989–90 edition, the Turbo Orlik has supplanted its predecessor in Polish Air Force planning. A new version of the aircraft, the PZL-130TB Turbo Orlik bis, is currently under development. This has a 29 ft 6⅓ in (9,00 m) wing span, an aerobatic version of the M 601E engine, crew ejection seats, longer-span double-slotted flaps, six underwing stores stations and a maximum take-off weight of 5,952 lb (2 700 kg). A decision was taken in 1989 to discontinue development of the piston-engined Orlik in favour of the Turbo Orlik, and five of the first production batch of 10 aircraft have been delivered to the Polish Air Force. The PT6A version is intended for export.

PZL-130TM TURBO ORLIK

Dimensions: Span, 26 ft 3 in (8,00 m); length, 28 ft 7¾ in (8,73 m); height, 11 ft 7 in (3,53 m); wing area, 132·18 sq ft (12,28 m²).

ROCKWELL B-1B LANCER

Country of Origin: USA.

Type: Strategic bomber and cruise missile carrier.

Power Plant: Four 30,780 lb st (136·9 kN) General Electric F101-GE-102 turbofans.

Performance: Max speed (without external ordnance), 795 mph (1 280 km/h) above 36,000 ft (10 975 m), or Mach = 1·25; low-level penetration speed, 610 mph (980 km/h), or Mach = 0·8; approx unrefuelled range, 7,500 mls (12 070 km).

Weights: Empty, 184,300 lb (83 500 kg); empty equipped, 192,000 lb (87 090 kg); max take-off, 477,000 lb (216 367 kg).

Accommodation: Flight crew of four comprising pilot, co-pilot/navigator, and defensive and offensive systems operators.

Armament: Three fuselage weapons bays to accommodate up to 84 Mk 82 500-lb (227-kg), 24 Mk 84 2,000-lb (908-kg) or B-83 2,439-lb (1 106-kg) bombs, or eight AGM-86B cruise missiles plus 12 AGM-69 defence suppression missiles. Up to 44 Mk 82 bombs or 14 720-lb (327-kg) B-61 nuclear bombs, or 14 AGM-86B missiles on six external stores stations beneath fuselage.

Status: First of 100 production B-1Bs flown on 18 October 1984, with initial deliveries to the USAF commencing on 29 June 1985, and final aircraft delivered on 30 April 1988. Officially named Lancer in May 1990.

Notes: The B-1B is an extensively revised derivative of the B-1A, the first of four prototypes of which first flew on 23 December 1974, two of these subsequently being converted to B-1B standards. By comparison with the B-1A, the B-1B has fixed engine air intakes, uses radar absorbent material in certain areas of the airframe, and offers a reduced radar signature. During the summer of 1987, the B-1B Lancer established a series of international speed and distance with payload records, but these have since been beaten by the Tupolev Tu-160 Blackjack.

ROCKWELL B-1B LANCER

Dimensions: Span (15 deg sweep), 136 ft 8½ in (41,67 m), (67·5 deg sweep), 78 ft 2½ in (23,84 m); length, 147 ft 0 in (44,81 m); height, 34 ft 0 in (10,36 m); wing area (approx), 1,950 sq ft (181,20 m²).

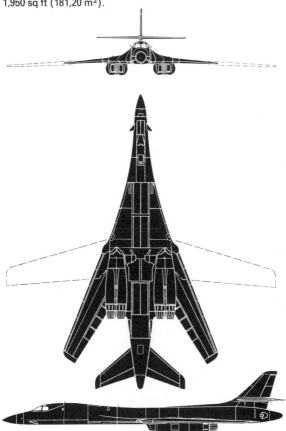

ROCKWELL/MBB X-31A

Countries of Origin: USA and Germany.
Type: Fighter manoeuvrability demonstration aircraft.
Power Plant: One 10,600 lb st (47·17 kN) dry and 15,800 lb st (70·28 kN) General Electric F404-GE-400 turbofan.
Performance: Max speed, 858 mph (1 380 km/h) at 40,000 ft (12 190 m), or Mach = 1·3; max initial climb, 43,000 ft/min (218,4 m/sec); max operating altitude, 40,000 ft (12 190 m).
Weights: Empty equipped, 11,410 lb (5 175 kg); normal loaded weight, 14,600 lb (6 622 kg); max take-off, 15,099 lb (6 849 kg).
Status: First of two flight demonstrators commenced flight test programme on 11 October 1990, with second following on 19 January 1991. The demonstration programme is scheduled to end early in 1992.
Notes: Intended as a research tool for use in the EFM (Enhanced Fighter Manoeuvrability) programme, the X-31A is the first of the US X-series aircraft to be developed jointly with another country. The participating companies are Rockwell International of the USA and the Messerschmitt-Bölkow-Blohm component of Deutsche Aerospace of Germany, the X-31A being funded jointly by the US (75 per cent) and German governments. This aircraft is intended to integrate several technologies, and will demonstrate the use of foreplanes and thrust vectoring to achieve controlled flight beyond the stall barrier, performing extremely tight turns at high angles of attack (in excess of 60 deg). The test schedule calls for 80 envelope-expansion flights, 200 post-stall demonstrations and 120 simulated combat sorties on instrumented ranges, the data generated being intended for use in future fighter design. The first flight with thrust-vectoring paddles took place on 14 February 1991.

ROCKWELL/MBB X-31A

Dimensions: Span, 23 ft 10 in (7,26 m); length (excluding probe), 43 ft 2 in (13,21 m); height, 14 ft 7 in (4,44 m); wing area, 226·3 sq ft (21,02 m²).

SAAB 39 GRIPEN

Country of Origin: Sweden.

Type: Single-seat multi-role fighter.

Power Plant: One 12,250 lb st (54·5 kN) dry and 18,100 lb st (80·5 kN) General Electric/Volvo Flygmotor RM 12 (F-404-400) turbofan.

Performance: No data have been released at the time of closing for press, but maximum speed is expected to range from 914 mph (1 470 km/h) at sea level, or Mach = 1·2, to 1,450 mph (2 555 km/h) above 36,000 ft (10 975 m), or Mach = 2·2.

Weights: Estimated clean loaded, 17,635 lb (8 000 kg).

Armament: One 27-mm Mauser BK 27 cannon and (intercept) four Rb 72 Sky Flash and two Rb 24 Sidewinder AAMs, or (attack) various electro-optically-guided ASMs, conventional or retarded bombs, or RBS 15F anti-shipping missiles.

Status: First of five prototypes flown on 9 December 1988 (this being lost in February 1989), the second prototype following on 4 May 1990. The fourth prototype flew on 20 December 1990, and the third and fifth are due to fly during the course of 1991. Initial contract for 30 series aircraft with deliveries scheduled to commence 1993, and a decision on a second contract for 110 aircraft expected to be taken during the course of 1991.

Notes: Designed to fulfil fighter, attack and reconnaissance tasks, all necessary hardware and software for these missions being carried permanently, the Gripen (Griffon) is officially designated JAS 39 by the Swedish Air Force, the prefix letters signifying its three roles (*Jakt/Attack/Spaning*). A design study of a tandem two-seat tactical training version, the JAS 39B, was authorised in July 1989, and some of the second contract Gripens may be completed to this standard. Making extensive use of composites, the Gripen features a triple-redundant digital fly-by-wire flight control system. An improved version, the JAS 39C, is being proposed for a third series production batch.

SAAB 39 GRIPEN

Dimensions: (Approximate) Span, 26 ft 3 in (8,00 m); length, 46 ft 3 in (14,00 m); height, 15 ft 5 in (4,70 m).

SAAB 340B

Country of Origin: Sweden.

Type: Regional commercial and corporate transport.

Power Plant: Two 1,870 hp (1,394 kW) General Electric CT7-9B turboprops.

Performance: Max cruise speed, 325 mph (522 km/h) at 15,000 ft (4 575 m), 322 mph (519 km/h) at 20,000 ft (6 100 m); range cruise, 290 mph (467 km/h) at 25,000 ft (7 620 m); max initial climb, 2,050 ft/min (10,41 m/sec); range with 45 min reserves (35 passengers), 1,123 mls (1 807 km), (30 passengers), 1,509 mls (2 427 km) at range cruise.

Weights: Operational empty, 17,715 lb (8 036 kg); max take-off, 28,500 lb (12 927 kg).

Accommodation: Flight crew of two and optional regional airline seating arrangements for 33, 35 or 37 passengers three abreast.

Status: First (SF 340) prototype flown 25 January 1983 and first production (4th aircraft) 340A flown on 5 March 1984. Production switched from 340A to 340B in August 1989 at No 160, initial delivery of the latter taking place in the following September. Deliveries of the 340A and B totalled 214 by the beginning of 1991 when firm orders had been placed for 330 aircraft and production was running at 55 annually.

Notes: The 340B is a 'hot and high' version of the 340A, and at the beginning of 1991 full scale development of a stretched version, the Saab 2000, was continuing with the first of three prototypes to fly early 1992. A total of 189 orders and options for the Saab 2000 had been received by the beginning of 1991. This will accommodate up to 58 passengers in high-density configuration.

Dimensions: Span, 70 ft 4 in (21,44 m); length, 64 ft 8$\frac{1}{2}$ in (19,72 m); height, 22 ft 6 in (6,86 m); wing area, 450 sq ft (41,81 m²).

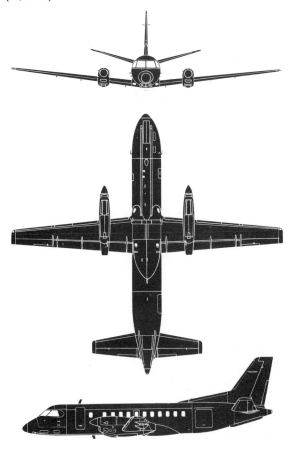

SHORTS C-23B SUPER SHERPA

Country of Origin: United Kingdom.
Type: Light freighter and utility aircraft.
Power Plant: Two 1,424 shp (1,062 kW) Pratt & Whitney Canada PT6A-65AR turboprops.
Performance: Max cruise speed (at 25,600 lb/11 612 kg), 224 mph (361 km/h); range cruise, 185 mph (298 km/h); range (with 7,280-lb/3 302-kg payload), 460 mls (740 km) with 45 min hold at 5,000 ft (1 525 m), (with 5,180-lb/2 350-kg payload), 1,010 mls (1 625 km).
Weights: Empty (freighter), 16,040 lb (7 276 kg), (trooper), 16,874 lb (7 654 kg); max take-off, 25,600 lb (11 612 kg).
Accommodation: Flight crew of two and (personnel transport) 30 passengers three abreast, (medevac) 15 casualty stretchers and three medical attendants, (paratroop transport) 27 paratroops on side-facing seats plus jumpmaster/dispatcher, or (freighter) 7,280 lb (3 302 kg) of cargo.
Status: First of 10 C-23Bs for US Army National Guard flown on 12 June 1990. Prototype Sherpa flown on 23 December 1982, and first of 18 ordered by the USAF (as C-23A) flown on 6 August 1984 and the last being delivered on 6 December 1985.
Notes: The Sherpa and Super Sherpa are freighter versions of the Shorts 330-200 30-passenger commercial transport, retaining many features of the all-passenger model to permit utility passenger transport operations. Their design incorporates a full-width dual-hinged ventral door which, serving as a ramp, may be opened inwards for supply dropping and permits through loading on the ground. The C-23A Sherpa was originally procured by the USAF to fulfil its EDSA (European Distribution System Aircraft) requirement, the C-23B Super Sherpa differing primarily in having cabin windows and uprated engines.

SHORTS C-23B SUPER SHERPA

Dimensions: Span, 74 ft 10 in (22,81 m); length, 58 ft 0½ in (17,69 m); height, 16 ft 4⅞ in (5,00 m); wing area, 453 sq ft (42,10 m²).

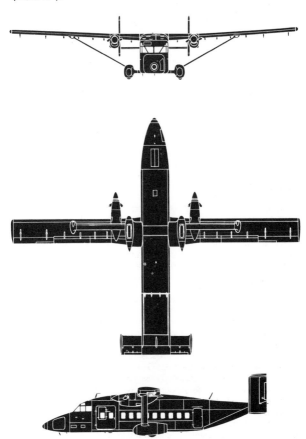

SHORTS S312 TUCANO

Country of Origin: United Kingdom (Brazil).
Type: Tandem two-seat basic trainer.
Power Plant: One 1,100 shp (820 kW) Garrett TPE331-12B turboprop.
Performance: Max speed (at 5,732 lb/2 600 kg), 315 mph (507 km/h) at 10,000–15,000 ft (3 050–4 575 m); normal cruise, 276 mph (448 km/h); econ cruise, 253 mph (407 km/h); max initial climb, 3,510 ft/min (17,38 m/sec); range (with 30 min reserves), 1,035 mls (1 665 km), (with external fuel), 2,061 mls (3 317 km) at 25,000 ft (7 620 m).
Weights: Basic empty (aerobatic), 4,447 lb (2 017 kg); max take-off (aerobatic), 6,393 lb (2 900 kg), (weapons configuration), 7,716 lb (3 500 kg).
Status: Brazilian-built prototype flown on 14 February 1986, with first Shorts-built aircraft following on 30 December, deliveries to the RAF (against order for 130) commencing on 16 June 1988, with approximately 75 delivered by beginning of 1991. In addition, 12 have been supplied to Kenya (as T Mk 51s) and 16 to Kuwait (as T Mk 52s).
Notes: Derived from the EMB-312 (see pages 106–7) specially to meet an RAF requirement, the S312 Tucano T Mk 1 has a more powerful engine, structural strengthening to extend the fatigue life, a ventral air brake and a revised cockpit layout. Kenyan Tucano T Mk 51s are armed and used for weapons training. The Shorts-built Tucano and that produced by Embraer possess only 25 per cent commonality.

SHORTS S312 TUCANO

Dimensions: Span, 37 ft 0 in (11,28 m); length, 32 ft 4$\frac{1}{4}$ in (9,86 m); height, 11 ft 1$\frac{7}{8}$ in (3,40 m); wing area, 208·07 sq ft (19,33 m²).

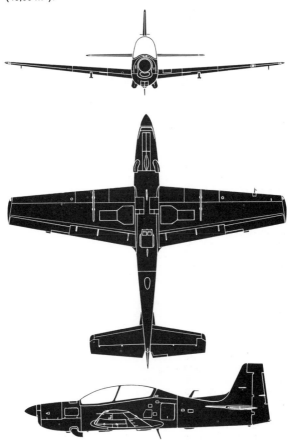

SIAI MARCHETTI S.211

Country of Origin: Italy.

Type: Tandem two-seat basic trainer.

Power Plant: One 2,500 lb st (11·13 kN) Pratt & Whitney Canada JT15D-4C turbofan.

Performance: Max speed, 414 mph (667 km/h) at 25,000 ft (7 620 m); range cruise, 311 mph (500 km/h) at 30,000 ft (9 150 m); max initial climb, 4,200 ft/min (21,34 m/sec); service ceiling, 40,000 ft (12 200 m); max range (internal fuel), 1,036 mls (1 668 km); ferry range (two 77 Imp gal/350 l external tanks), 1,543 mls (2 483 km).

Weights: Empty, 3,968 lb (1 800 kg); max take-off (training mission), 6,063 lb (2 750 kg), (with armament), 6,944 lb (3 150 kg).

Armament: (Weapons training and light attack) Four wing stations each stressed for 727·5 lb (330 kg) inboard and 364 lb (165 kg) outboard. Max external ordnance load of 1,455 lb (660 kg). Typical loads can include two 20-mm or four 12,7-mm gun pods, four 18 × 50-mm, 7 × 2·75-in or 6 × 68-mm rockets, or four bombs each of up to 330 lb (150 kg).

Status: First of three prototypes flown 10 April 1981, and first production aircraft (for Singapore) flown on 4 October 1984. Customers include Philippines (18), Singapore (30) and Haiti (4). Philippine aircraft assembled by Philippines Aerospace Development Corporation after delivery in CKD form. First six for Singapore delivered in CKD kit form with further 23 built by SAMCO.

194

SIAI MARCHETTI S.211

Dimensions: Span, 27 ft 8 in (8,43 m); length, 30 ft 6½ in (9,31 m); height, 12 ft 5½ in (3,80 m); wing area, 135·63 sq ft (12,60 m²).

SOCATA TB 31 OMÉGA

Country of Origin: France.
Type: Tandem two-seat basic trainer.
Power Plant: One 488 shp (364 kW) Turboméca TP 319 1A2 turboprop derated to 360 shp (268 kW).
Performance: Max speed, 322 mph (519 km/h) at sea level; max cruise, 269 mph (434 km/h) at 10,000 ft (3 050 m); econ cruise, 220 mph (354 km/h); max initial climb, 2,100 ft/min (10,67 m/sec); service ceiling, 30,000 ft (9 145 m); range (75% power with 20 min reserves), 813 mls (1 308 km).
Weights: Empty equipped, 1,896 lb (860 kg); max take-off, 3,086 lb (1 400 kg).
Status: The prototype Oméga (an adaptation of the Epsilon TP 319 testbed) was first flown on 30 April 1989. No production contracts had been announced by the beginning of 1991.
Notes: The Oméga is a derivative of the TB 30 Epsilon (see previous edition) in which a turboprop replaces the Textron Lycoming AEIO-540-L1B5D piston engine and lightweight ejection seats (an optional feature) are provided beneath a new, two-piece canopy. The Oméga shares approximately 60 per cent of its structural components with the Epsilon, and offers greater fatigue tolerance and a wider manoeuvre envelope. Similar armament provisions to those of the Epsilon export model are available. The Epsilon (handled by the Aircraft Division of Aérospatiale until 1989) has been supplied to the *Armée de l'Air* (150), Portugal (18) and Togo (4).

SOCATA TB 31 OMÉGA

Dimensions: Span, 25 ft 11¾ in (7,92 m); length, 25 ft 7½ in (7,81 m); height, 8 ft 9½ in (2,68 m); wing area, 96·9 sq ft (9,00 m²).

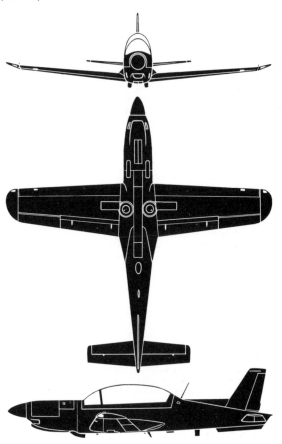

SUKHOI SU-24 (FENCER)

Country of Origin: USSR.

Type: Two-seat deep penetration interdictor and strike, reconnaissance and electronic warfare aircraft.

Power Plant: Two 24,700 lb st (110 kN) reheat Saturn (Lyulka) AL-21F-3A turbojets.

Performance: (Su-24MK) Max speed (clean), 1,440 mph (2 317 km/h) above 36,090 ft (11 000 m), or Mach = 2·18, 820 mph (1 320 km/h) at 4,920 ft (1 500 m), or Mach = 1·15; service ceiling, 57,400 ft (17 500 m); tactical radius (HI-LO-HI with two 275 Imp gal/1 250 l drop tanks and 6,615 lb/3 000 kg ordnance), 650 mls (1 050 km), (LO-LO-HI with 5,500 lb ordnance), 590 mls (950 km), (LO-LO-LO), 200+ mls (320+ km).

Weights: Empty equipped, 41,885 lb (19 000 kg); normal loaded, 79,365 lb (36 000 kg); max take-off, 87,523 lb (39 700 kg).

Armament: Maximum external stores load of 17,635 lb (8 000 kg) plus one six-barrel 30-mm rotary cannon. Four fuselage and four wing stations capable of carrying a variety of weaponry, including AS-7 Kerry, AS-10 Karen, AS-11 Kilter, AS-12 Kegler, AS-13 Kinbolt and AS-14 Kedge air-to-surface missiles.

Status: Both fixed- and variable-geometry prototypes were flown in 1969, the fixed-geometry prototypes (T-60 and T-61) being discarded in favour of the variable-geometry (T-62) aircraft, the production derivative of which attained initial operational status from late 1974. At the beginning of 1991, more than 800 (including 500 assigned to the strategic role) were serving with the SovAF and some 60 with Soviet naval aviation. Exports have included Iraq (10), Libya (15) and Syria (12).

Notes: The Su-24MK (Fencer-D) introduced in 1983 and illustrated here is numerically the most important version of this type.

SUKHOI SU-24 (FENCER)

Dimensions: Span (16 deg sweep), 57 ft 10 in (17,63 m), (68 deg sweep), 34 ft 0 in (10,36 m); length (including probe), 80 ft 5¾ in (24,53 m); height, 16 ft 3¾ in (4,97 m); wing area, 452 sq ft (42,00 m²).

SUKHOI SU-25 (FROGFOOT)

Country of Origin: USSR.
Type: Single-seat (Su-25K) close air support and (Su-25UB) two-seat operational conversion and weapons training aircraft.
Power Plant: Two 9,921 lb st (44·18 kN) Tumansky R-195 turbojets.
Performance: (Su-25K) Max speed, 606 mph (975 km/h) at sea level, or Mach = 0·8; service ceiling, 22,965 ft (7 000 m); range with 9,700-lb (4 400-kg) ordnance load and two external tanks, 466 mls (750 km) at sea level, 776 mls (1 250 km) at altitude.
Weights: (Su-25K) Empty equipped, 20,950 lb (9 500 kg); normal loaded, 32,187 lb (14 600 kg); max take-off, 38,800 lb (17 600 kg).
Armament: One twin-barrel 30-mm cannon and up to 9,700 lb (4 400 kg) of ordnance distributed between eight wing pylons. Two additional wing pylons outboard for two R-60 Aphid self-defence AAMs.
Status: Prototype flown 22 February 1975, with production following from 1978, full operational capability being achieved in 1984. Exported to Afghanistan, Bulgaria, Czechoslovakia and Iraq. Some 250–300 in SovAF service at the beginning of 1991.
Notes: Single-seat Su-25K (Frogfoot-A) illustrated above and two-seat Su-25UB (Frogfoot-B) on opposite page, the export version of the latter being designated Su-28. The Su-28, also known as the Su-25UT, was first flown on 6 August 1985, and lacks the arrester hook of the Su-25UB. A navalised version of the Su-25 is under development for service aboard the carriers *Kuznetsov* and *Varyag* (formerly *Tbilisi* and *Riga*).

SUKHOI SU-25 (FROGFOOT)

Dimensions: (Su-25UB) Span, 47 ft 1½ in (13,36 m); length, 50 ft 4¾ in (15,36 m); height, 15 ft 9 in (4,80 m); wing area, 362·75 sq ft (33,70 m²).

SUKHOI SU-27 (FLANKER)

Country of Origin: USSR.

Type: Single-seat all-weather counterair fighter.

Power Plant: Two 27,575 lb st (123·85 kN) reheat Saturn (Lyulka) AL-31F turbofans.

Performance: Max speed, 1,550 mph (2 500 km/h) above 36,100 ft (11 000 m), or Mach = 2·35, 835 mph (1 345 km/h) at sea level, or Mach = 1·1; service ceiling, 59,055 ft (18 000 m); combat radius (subsonic intercept mission with four R-27 and four R-73 AAMs), 930 mls (1 500 km); range (with max fuel), 2,485 mls (4 000 km).

Weights: Normal loaded, 48,500 lb (22 000 kg); max take-off, 66,135 lb (30 000 kg).

Armament: One 30-mm six-barrel rotary cannon and up to 10 AAMs on fuselage tandem pylons, beneath the engine ducts, beneath the outer wings and at each wing tip, a typical mix comprising four R-60 Aphid or R-73 Archer close-range IR missiles and six R-27 Alamo (two short-burn semi-active radar Alamo-A, two short-burn IR-homing Alamo-B and two long-burn semi-active radar Alamo-C) medium- and long-range AAMs.

Status: Prototype (T-10) flown on 20 May 1977, followed by extensively redesigned prototype on 20 April 1981, this (Flanker-B) entering production in 1982–83 at Komsomolsk with initial operational capability achieved 1986.

Notes: The two-seat Su-27UB Flanker-C (seen in background above) is a conversion trainer retaining full combat capability. A version for ramp-assisted operation from Soviet aircraft carriers has folding outer wing panels, foreplanes, revised undercarriage, arrester hook and flight refuelling capability. Tests have been performed aboard the carrier *Kuznetsov*.

SUKHOI SU-27 (FLANKER)

Dimensions: Span, 48 ft 2¾ in (14,70 m); length (excluding probe), 71 ft 11½ in (21,93 m); height, 19 ft 5½ in (5,93 m); wing area (approx), 680 sq ft (63,20 m²).

SWEARINGEN (JAFFE) SA-32T TURBO TRAINER

Country of Origin: USA.

Type: Side-by-side two-seat basic trainer.

Power Plant: One 420 shp (313 kW) Allison 250-B-17D turboprop.

Performance: (At 2,600 lb/1 179 kg) Max speed, 332 mph (534 km/h) at sea level; normal cruise (75% power), 315 mph (508 km/h) at 20,000 ft (6 100 m); max initial climb, 3,700 ft/min (18,8 m/sec); service ceiling, 25,000+ ft (7 620+ m); max range (no reserves), 1,105 mls (1 779 km).

Weights: Empty (typical), 1,560 lb (708 kg); max take-off, 2,600 lb (1 179 kg).

Status: First prototype flown on 31 May 1989, and second prototype featuring tandem seating expected to enter flight test late 1991. Both side-by-side and tandem seat versions are to be offered in kit form for assembly in Third World countries.

Notes: Designed by Edward J Swearingen of Swearingen Engineering and Technology, and developed in conjunction with the Jaffe Aircraft Corporation, the SA-32T Turbo Trainer is a military tuitional derivative of the SX300 high-performance two-seater, which, powered by a 300 hp Textron Lycoming IO-540 piston engine, established FAI-recognised international speed records in the C1b and C1c classes. The SA-32T employs the same low-drag laminar flow aerofoil and simulates the flying behaviour of jet aircraft to which the pupil pilot will transition. Other features of the SA-32T accord with the philosophy that the pupil should be introduced to fighter-like handling at the earliest possible tuitional phase. The narrow-track undercarriage, for example, has been patterned on the landing gear of latest-generation fighters and may be extended at jet approach speeds. McDonnell Douglas MiniPack ejection seats are being considered for the tandem-seat version.

SWEARINGEN (JAFFE) SA-32T TURBO TRAINER

Dimensions: Span, 24 ft 4½ in (7,44 m); length, 22 ft 6 in (6,86 m); height, 7 ft 9¼ in (2,38 m); wing area, 71·5 sq ft (6,64 m²).

SWEARINGEN-JAFFE SJ30

Country of Origin: USA.

Type: Light corporate executive transport.

Power Plant: Two 1,900 lb st (8·6 kN) Williams International FJ44 turbofans.

Performance: (Manufacturer's estimates) Max cruise speed, 512 mph (824 km/h), or Mach = 0·77; range cruise, 475 mph (765 km/h), or Mach = 0·72; max operating altitude, 41,000 ft (12 500 m); max range (IFR), 1,990 mls (3 205 km), (VFR), 2,390 mls (3 845 km).

Weights: Empty equipped, 5,700 lb (2 586 kg); max take-off, 9,850 lb (4 469 kg).

Accommodation: Pilot and co-pilot/passenger on flight deck and standard main cabin arrangement for four passengers in individual seats in facing pairs. Optional arrangements for up to six passengers.

Status: First prototype entered flight test on 13 February 1991, and second (series) prototype for certification expected to join development programme late year. Certification anticipated late 1992, with first deliveries following before year's end.

Notes: An advanced-technology 'low cost' corporate transport intended to compete with turboprop-powered aircraft of similar capacity, the SJ30 developed by Swearingen Engineering and Technology was to have been marketed by Gulfstream Aerospace as the SA-30 Gulfjet. Gulfstream withdrew from the project on 1 September 1989, its place being taken by the Jaffe Group. The refinancing that this necessitated together with various design changes that were found necessary before the commencement of flight testing have combined to delay the programme by some 18–24 months. The SJ30 is in direct competition with the similarly-powered CitationJet.

SWEARINGEN-JAFFE SJ30

Dimensions: Span, 36 ft 4 in (11,07 m); length, 42 ft $3\frac{7}{8}$ in (12,89 m); height, 12 ft 11 in (3,94 m); wing area, 164·9 sq ft (15,32 m²).

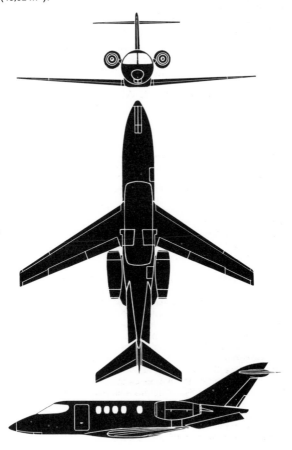

TBM SA TBM 700

Countries of Origin: France and USA.
Type: Light business and executive transport.
Power Plant: One 700 shp (522 kW) Pratt & Whitney Canada PT6A-64 turboprop.
Performance: Max speed, 345 mph (556 km/h) at 26,000 ft (7 925 m); max cruise, 333 mph (536 km/h) at 30,000 ft (9 145 m); normal cruise, 325 mph (523 km/h) at 30,000 ft (9 145 m); range cruise, 281 mph (452 km/h) at 30,000 ft (9 145 m); max range (six passengers), 1,180 mls (1 900 km), (max fuel), 1,925 mls (3 100 km).
Weights: Standard empty, 3,946 lb (1 790 kg); max take-off, 6,580 lb (2 985 kg).
Accommodation: Pilot and co-pilot/passenger on flight deck and up to six passengers in main cabin, typical arrangement being for four passengers with club seating.
Status: First of three prototypes flown on 14 July 1988, with second and third following on 3 August and 11 October 1989. First production aircraft flown on 24 August 1990 in France. Production by Socata (France) one per month at beginning of 1991 when orders exceeded 70 aircraft. Assembly in the USA (by Mooney) commencing in 1991, and manufacture of six aircraft monthly (by the two assembly lines) expected by 1992.
Notes: The TBM 700 has been developed in France by Socata (two-thirds) and the USA by Mooney (one-third), the former manufacturing cabin, tailplane, fin, ailerons and flaps, and the latter building the rear fuselage. The TMB SA is an association created jointly by Socata and Mooney.

TBM SA TBM 700

Dimensions: Span, 39 ft 10¾ in (12,16 m); length, 34 ft 2½ in (10,43 m); height, 13 ft 1 in (3,99 m); wing area, 193·7 sq ft (18,00 m²).

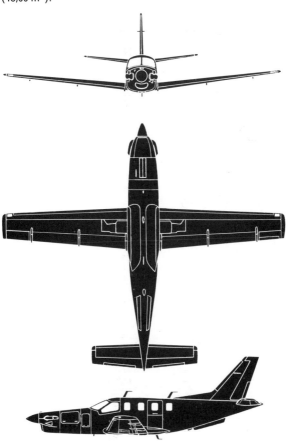

TUPOLEV TU-26 (BACKFIRE-C)

Country of Origin: USSR.

Type: Medium-range strategic bomber and maritime strike/reconnaissance aircraft.

Power Plant: Two (estimated) 35,000 lb st (155·67 kN) dry and 50,000 lb st (222·27 kN) reheat KKBM (Kuznetsov) turbofans.

Performance: (Estimated) Max speed (short period dash), 1,320 mph (2 124 km/h) at 39,370 ft (12 000 m), or Mach = 2·0, (sustained), 1,090 mph (1 755 km/h), or Mach = 1·65; combat radius (unrefuelled high-altitude subsonic mission profile), 2,160 mls (4 200 km).

Weights: (Estimated) Max take-off, 285 000 lb (129 275 kg).

Armament: One twin-barrel 23-mm cannon in remotely-controlled tail barbette. Primary armament of two AS-4 Kitchen inertially-guided stand-off missiles on wing centre section pylons or one AS-4 semi-recessed on fuselage centreline, plus AS-9 Kyle anti-radar missiles. Maximum internal load of conventional bombs, 26,460 lb (12 000 kg).

Status: The Tu-26 (alias Tu-22M) is believed to have entered flight test in 1971, a pre-series (Backfire-A) undergoing service evaluation in 1973, and initial series version (Backfire-B) achieving initial operational capability in 1977–78, with advanced version (Backfire-C) following in service from 1985. In excess of 400 Backfire-B and -C bomber, reconnaissance and electronic warfare aircraft in service with the SovAF at the beginning of 1991, and some 150 with the Soviet Navy. Production continuing at approx 30 annually.

Notes: The Backfire-C differs externally from the -B primarily in having a larger, recontoured nose radome and larger, wedge-type engine air intakes. Current production is primarily for the naval air component.

TUPOLEV TU-26 (BACKFIRE-C)

Dimensions: (Estimated) Span (20 deg sweep), 112 ft 6 in (34,30 m), (65 deg sweep), 76 ft 9 in (23,40 m); length, 130 ft 0 in (39,62 m); height, 35 ft 5$\frac{1}{4}$ in (10,80 m); wing area, 1,800 sq ft (167,22 m²).

TUPOLEV TU-160 (BLACKJACK-A)

Country of Origin: USSR.

Type: Long-range strategic bomber and maritime strike/reconnaissance aircraft.

Power Plant: Four 55,115 lb st (245·14 kN) reheat Type 'R' turbofans.

Performance: Max (over-target dash) speed, 1,366 mph (2 200 km/h) at 36,090 ft (11 000 m), or Mach = 2·07; max continuous cruise, 1,056 mph (1 700 km/h), or Mach = 1·6; range cruise, 595 mph (960 km/h) at 45,930 ft (14 000 m), or Mach = 0·9; normal max range (unrefuelled), 4,535 mls (7 300 km).

Weights: Max take-off, 606,260 lb (275 000 kg).

Armament: Two 32·8-ft (10,00-m) weapons bays with rotary dispensers capable of carrying a total of 35,935 lb (16 300 kg) of ordnance. Alternative internal loads include 12 1,865-mile (3 000-km) range AS-15 Kent subsonic low-altitude cruise missiles, 24 AS-16 (BL-10) supersonic short-range attack missiles or (from 1992) an unspecified number of AS-19 supersonic cruise missiles.

Status: Designed under the leadership of V Bliznyuk through the *Samolyot* (Aircraft) 70 programme, the Tu-160 entered flight test in 1982, with series production commencing at Kazan in 1984–85, and peaking at 30 aircraft per annum by beginning of 1991. The first SovAF Tu-160 squadron formed mid-1988 at Dolon AB, Central USSR.

Notes: The 14th production Tu-160 (referred to as *Samolyot* 70-03) made two record-breaking flights on 31 October and 3 November 1989, a number of closed-circuit speed-with-load and altitude-with-load records being submitted to the FAI.

TUPOLEV TU-160 (BLACKJACK-A)

Dimensions: Span (20 deg sweep), 182 ft 9 in (55,70 m), (65 deg sweep), 110 ft 9 in (33,75 m); length, 177 ft 2 in (54,00 m); height, 42 ft 0 in (12,80 m).

TUPOLEV TU-204-100

Country of Origin: USSR.

Type: Medium-haul commercial transport.

Power Plant: Two 35,275 lb st (156·9 kN) Perm (Soloviev) PS-90A turbofans.

Performance: (At 206,125 lb/93 500 kg) Max cruise speed, 528 mph (850 km/h) at 35,000 ft (10 650 m); econ cruise, 503 mph (810 km/h) at 40,000 ft (12 200 m); range (with 196 passengers), 2,392 mls (3 850 km) at 515 mph (828 km/h) at 36,100 ft (11 000 m).

Weights: Operational empty, 124,560 lb (56 500 kg); max take-off, 219,356 lb (99 500 kg).

Accommodation: Flight crew of two (with optional flight engineer) with maximum of 214 passengers four abreast in all-economy class arrangement. Other basic single-aisle arrangements are 12 first-class four abreast and 35 business-class and 143 economy-class passengers six abreast, and 12 first-class four abreast and 184 economy-class passengers six abreast.

Status: First of two prototypes flown on 2 January 1989, and first pre-production aircraft flown August 1990, with two more completed by beginning of 1991. Aeroflot requirement for 350 aircraft of this type with service entry anticipated late 1991.

Notes: The Soviet counterpart to the Boeing 757, the Tu-204 has triple inertial navigation systems and a wing of super-critical section. The -100 scheduled to be followed by -200 with a maximum weight of 239,200 lb (108 500 kg). At the beginning of 1991 consideration was being given to powering a version of the -200 with Pratt & Whitney PW2037 turbofans which could be certified in the mid 'nineties. Longer-range versions currently planned are the Tu-204-100M offering a range of 3,293 mls (5 300 km) and the Tu-204-200M with a range of 4,460 mls (7 180 km).

TUPOLEV TU-204-100

Dimensions: Span, 137 ft 9½ in (42,00 m); length, 151 ft 7¾ in (46,22 m); height, 45 ft 6½ in (13,88 m); wing area, 1,982·5 sq ft (184,17 m²).

VALMET L-90 TP REDIGO

Country of Origin: Finland.

Type: Two/four-seat multi-purpose primary/basic training and liaison aircraft.

Power Plant: One 500 shp (373 kW) Allison 250-B17F turbo-prop flat rated at 420 shp (313 kW).

Performance: (At 2,976 lb/1 350 kg) Max speed, 208 mph (335 km/h) at 5,000 ft (1 525 m); cruise (75% power), 189 mph (305 km/h) at 9,840 ft (3 000 m); max initial climb, 1,930 ft/min (9,80 m/sec); time to 16,400 ft (5 000 m), 11·5 min; range, 932 mls (1 500 km) at 19,685 ft (6 000 m).

Weights: Empty equipped (aerobatic), 1,962 lb (890 kg); max take-off (aerobatic), 2,976 lb (1 350 kg), (utility with external stores), 4,189 lb (1 900 kg).

Armament: (Weapons training and light strike) Max external load of 1,764 lb (800 kg) distributed between six underwing stations, the two inboard stations each stressed for 551 lb (250 kg) and remaining four stressed for 331 lb (150 kg) each. Typical loads (when flown as single-seater) include four 330·5-lb (150-kg) bombs, or two 551-lb (250-kg) bombs and two flare pods.

Status: First of two prototypes flown on 1 July 1986, and second (with Turboméca TP 319 engine) on 3 December 1987. Deliveries against a Finnish Air Force contract for 10 aircraft scheduled to begin during course of 1991.

Notes: An enlarged, unswept vertical tail introduced during 1990 (see opposite page).

VALMET L-90 TP REDIGO

Dimensions: Span, 34 ft 0½ in (10,37 m); length, 25 ft 11 in (7,90 m); height, 9 ft 4¼ in (2,85 m); wing area, 158·77 sq ft (14,75 m²).

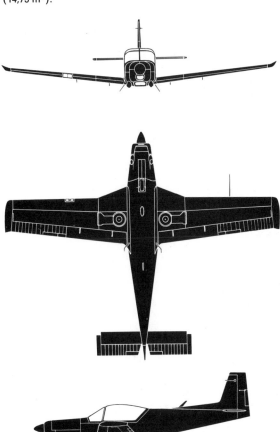

AEROSPATIALE AS 332/532
SUPER PUMA MK II/COUGAR

Country of Origin: France.
Type: Multi-role civil (AS 332) and military (AS 532) helicopter.
Power Plant: Two 1,843 shp (1,374 kW) Turboméca Makila 1A2 turboshafts with emergency rating of 1,959 shp (1 461 kW).
Performance: (AS 532) Max speed, 173 mph (278 km/h); cruise, 149 mph (240 km/h) at sea level; max inclined climb, 1,220 ft/min (6,2 m/sec); hovering ceiling (in ground effect), 8,856 ft (2 700 m), (out of ground effect), 5,248 ft (1 600 m); range (standard tankage), 541 mls (870 km).
Weights: Empty, 9,920 lb (4 500 kg); Max take-off, 19,840 lb (9 000 kg), (with slung load), 20,615 lb (9 350 kg).
Dimensions: Rotor diam, 51 ft 2½ in (15,60 m); fuselage length (tail rotor included), 50 ft 11⅓ in (15,53 m).
Notes: The AS 332 Super Puma Mk II and the AS 532 Cougar are respectively civil and military versions of the same basic helicopter. In the civil version maximum passenger capacity is 23 plus a flight attendant, while the military variant can accommodate 29 troops. The Super Puma Mk II development vehicle first flew on 6 February 1987. Current version of the Super Puma Mk II is the AS 332 L2, and versions of the Cougar on offer are the AS 532 MC and SC, respectively SAR and ASW models, the tactical support AS 532 UC with 20-mm cannon or rocket launchers, and the AS 532 U2 troop transport and medevac (six stretchers and six seated casualties/medical attendants) helicopter.

AEROSPATIALE AS 350/550
ECUREUIL/FENNEC

Country of Origin: France.

Type: Five/six-seat light general-purpose helicopter.

Power Plant: One 724 shp (540 kW) Turboméca Arriel 1D1 turboshaft.

Performance: (AS 550) Max speed, 178 mph (287 km/h); cruise, 155 mph (249 km/h) at sea level; max inclined climb, 1,988 ft/min (10,1 m/sec); hovering ceiling (in ground effect), 13,300 ft (4 050 m), (out of ground effect), 11,200 ft (3 400 m); range (standard tankage), 426 mls (686 km).

Weights: Empty, 2,601 lb (1 180 kg); max take-off (anti-tank configuration), 5,181 lb (2 350 kg), (with external load), 5,512 lb (2 500 kg).

Dimensions: Rotor diam, 35 ft 0¾ in (10,69 m); fuselage length (tail rotor included), 35 ft 10½ in (10,93 m).

Notes: The AS 350 Ecureuil and AS 550 Fennec are respectively civil and military versions of the same basic helicopter, more than 1,300 having been delivered by the beginning of 1991. A version powered by the Textron Lycoming LTS 101-600A-3 turboshaft is marketed in North America as the AStar and with the Arriel 1D1 as the SuperStar. The military Fennec is available as the AS 550 U2 utility transport, the AS 550 A2 fire support and aerial combat with airframe reinforcement for axial armament, and the AS 550 C2 anti-armour model with the Saab/Emerson Electric HeliTow anti-tank missile system. The AS 550 A2 makes provision for a wide range of weapons, including a 20-mm cannon and twin 7,62-mm gun pods.

AEROSPATIALE AS 355/555
ECUREUIL 2/FENNEC

Country of Origin: France.

Type: Five/six-seat light general-purpose helicopter.

Power Plant: Two 460 shp (343 kW) Allison 250-C20R turboshafts.

Performance: Max speed, 173 mph (278 km/h); cruise, 140 mph (225 km/h) at sea level; max inclined climb, 1,280 ft/min (6,5 m/sec); hovering ceiling (in ground effect), 8,200 ft (2 500 m), (out of ground effect), 4,987 ft (1 520 m); range (standard fuel), 445 mls (717 km) at sea level.

Weights: Empty, 3,432 lb (1 560 kg); max take-off, 5,600 lb (2 540 kg), (with external load), 5,732 lb (2 600 kg).

Dimensions: Rotor diam, 35 ft 0¾ in (10,69 m); fuselage length (tail rotor included), 35 ft 10⅓ in (10,93 m).

Notes: The AS 355 Ecureuil 2 and AS 555 Fennec are respectively designations for the civil and military versions of the same basic helicopter which first entered flight test on 27 September 1979, and of which more than 400 had been delivered by the beginning of 1991. The current production version of the Ecureuil (Squirrel) 2 is the AS 355 F2R and this is marketed in North America as the TwinStar. Military models are the utility AS 555 UR, the armed AS 555 AR with optional weapons including rocket or machine gun packs, a 20-mm cannon and HOT or TOW anti-tank missiles, the maritime patrol AS 555 MR and the ASW AS 555 SR (illustrated above). The AS 555 MN and SN are respectively maritime patrol and ASW versions powered by paired TM 319 engines.

AEROSPATIALE AS 365 N2 DAUPHIN 2

Country of Origin: France.
Type: Commercial 10/14-seat general-purpose helicopter.
Power Plant: Two 733 shp (547 kW) Turboméca Arriel 1C2 turboshafts.
Performance: Max speed, 184 mph (296 km/h); max cruise, 176 mph (283 km/h); econ cruise, 161 mph (260 km/h); max inclined climb, 1,379 ft/min (7,0 m/sec); hovering ceiling (in ground effect), 8,365 ft (2 550 m), (out of ground effect), 5,905 ft (1 800 m); range (standard fuel), 557 mls (897 km).
Weights: Empty equipped, 4,970 lb (2 254 kg); max take-off, 9,370 lb (4 250 kg).
Dimensions: Rotor diam, 39 ft 2 in (11,94 m); fuselage length (tail rotor included), 38 ft 1$\frac{7}{8}$ in (11,63 m).
Notes: The AS 365 was flown as a prototype on 31 March 1979, and the standard production version is currently the AS 365 N2 which features uprated turboshafts, increased maximum weight and redesigned doors, deliveries having commenced mid 1990. The AS 365 is licence-built in China as the Harbin Z-9, and a modified version for the US Coast Guard is designated AS 366G (HH-65A Dolphin). Deliveries of all versions of the Dauphin 2 (including Chinese-built helicopters) totalled some 500 by the beginning of 1991. The AS 366G, of which 99 have been supplied to the US Coast Guard, is powered by paired 680 shp (507 kW) Textron Lycoming LTS 101-750A-1 turboshafts, but flight testing of an example re-engined with a 1,200 shp (895 kW) T800 turboshaft was scheduled to commence early in 1991 with a view to replacing the LTS 101s.

AEROSPATIALE AS 565 PANTHER

Country of Origin: France.
Type: Multi-role light military helicopter.
Power Plant: Two 748 shp (558 kW) Turboméca Arriel 1M1 turboshafts.
Performance: Max speed, 184 mph (296 km/h), cruise, 172 mph (277 km/h) at sea level; max inclined climb, 1,378 ft/min (7,0 m/sec); hovering ceiling (in ground effect), 8,530 ft (2 600 m), (out of ground effect), 6,070 ft (1 850 m); range (with standard fuel), 544 mls (875 km) at sea level.
Weights: Empty, 4,835 lb (2 193 kg); max take-off, 9,369 lb (4 250 kg).
Dimensions: Rotor diam, 39 ft 2 in (11,94 m); fuselage length (including tail rotor), 39 ft 8¾ in (12,11 m).
Notes: A military development of the Dauphin 2 emphasising survivability in a combat environment, the AS 565 flew as a prototype on 29 February 1984. Composite materials are used exclusively for the dynamic components and to an increased extent (by comparison with the AS 365) in the fuselage structure. The crew seats are armoured as are the control servos and engine controls. A number of versions are on offer, these being the utility AS 565 UA, the anti-tank AS 565 CA, the aerial combat and ground attack AS 565 AA, the maritime patrol and SAR AS 565 MA and the ASW AS 565 SA. The AS 565 AA (illustrated above) has a 20-mm cannon, a launcher for 19 2·75-in rockets, two 22-round packs of 68-mm rockets, or four two-round packs of Mistral IR-homing AAMs. The AS 565 AA has been supplied to Angola and Brazil.

AGUSTA A 109K₂

Country of Origin: Italy.

Type: Light multi-role helicopter (for 'hot and high' operations).

Power Plant: Two 737 shp (550 kW) Turboméca Arriel 1K1 turboshafts.

Performance: (At 5,997 lb/2 720 kg) Max cruise speed, 163 mph (263 km/h); max inclined climb, 2,200 ft/min (11,18 m/sec); hovering ceiling (in ground effect), 17,800 ft (5 425 m), (out of ground effect), 14,600 ft (4 450 m); service ceiling, 20,000 ft (6 100 m); max range, 261 mls (420 km); max endurance, 3·5 hrs.

Weights: Empty, 3,573 lb (1 622 kg); loaded (clean), 5,997 lb (2 720 kg); max take-off (with external load), 6,283 lb (2 850 kg).

Dimensions: Rotor diam, 36 ft 1 in (11,00 m); fuselage length, 36 ft 5¼ in (11,11 m).

Notes: The A 109K₂ is a development of the A 109A Mk II specifically intended for 'hot and high' operations, Arriel turboshafts replacing the 420 shp (313 kW) Allison 250-C20Bs of other versions. A miliary version, the A 109KM, may be fitted with a HeliTow launch system for up to eight TOW wire-guided missiles, a pintle-mounted 7,62-mm gun and a door gunner post 12,7-mm gun. The A 109K₂ is one of several current versions of the A 109, which, first flown on 4 August 1971, has been in continuous production since 1974, the latest variant being the A 109C Executive offered from 1991. Manufacturing tempo was increasing at the beginning of 1991 from nine monthly to an estimated 16·5 in 1992.

AGUSTA A 129 MANGUSTA

Country of Origin: Italy.

Type: Two-seat light anti-armour, attack and scout helicopter.

Power Plant: Two 825 shp (615 kW) Rolls-Royce Gem 2 Mk 1004D turboshafts.

Performance: (At 8,488 lb/3 850 kg) Max speed, 171 mph (275 km/h) at sea level; max continuous cruise, 155 mph (250 km/h); max inclined climb, 2,025 ft/min (10·29 m/sec); hovering ceiling (in ground effect), 10,300 ft (3 140 m), (out of ground effect), 6,200 ft (1 890 m); max ceiling, 15,500 ft (4 725 m); range, 328 mls (528 km); endurance, 3·075 hrs.

Weights: Normal loaded (anti-armour configuration), 8,488 lb (3 850 kg); max take-off, 8,973 lb (4 070 kg).

Dimensions: Rotor diam, 39 ft 0½ in (11,90 m); fuselage length, 40 ft 3¼ in (12,27 m).

Notes: The Mangusta (Mongoose) has been developed to meet an Italian Army requirement, and the first of five flying prototypes entered flight test on 11 September 1983, but the first five production helicopters were not accepted by the Army until late 1990 when it was anticipated that a further 10 would be delivered during the course of 1991. The Army has a requirement for 60 Mangusta helicopters, but contracts for only 15 had been placed by the beginning of 1991. The Mangusta has four stores stations beneath its stub wings, all stressed for loads up to 661 lb (300 kg), and basic armament is provided by TOW anti-armour missiles with a Saab/Emerson HeliTOW launch system, two, three or four of these wire-guided weapons being housed in a pod suspended from each wingtip station.

ATLAS XH-2 ROOIVALK

Country of Origin: South Africa.
Type: Tandem two-seat ground support and escort helicopter.
Power Plant: Two 1,575 shp (1,175 kW) Turboméca Turmo IVC turboshafts.
Performance: Max cruise speed, 167+ mph (269+ km/h); max inclined climb, 1,100 ft/min (5·59 m/sec); hovering ceiling (in ground effect), 7,545 ft (2 300 m); max range (at normal cruise with 30 min reserves), 460 mls (740 km).
Weights: Max take-off, 17,637+ lb (8 000+ kg).
Dimensions: Rotor diam, 49 ft 5¾ in (15,08 m); overall length, 54 ft 7½ in (16,65 m).
Notes: The Rooivalk (Rock Kestrel) was designed to meet a requirement formulated by the South African Air Force in 1984. Following the virtual cessation of armed conflict on South Africa's borders and defence cuts as a consequence, the service was forced to remove the Rooivalk from planned procurement, but the Atlas Aircraft Corporation was continuing development at the beginning of 1991 when export orders for the helicopter were being sought. First flown on 11 February 1990, the Rooivalk makes use of the dynamics of the Aérospatiale SA 330 Puma with the notable exception of the engine position. In order to provide the pilot (in the rear cockpit) with an unimpeded field of view, the Turmo engines were moved aft, necessitating new transmission design. Armament includes a turreted GAF-1 20-mm cannon, podded 68-mm unguided rockets and V3B Kukri or all-aspect Darter AAMs for self defence.

BELL MODEL 406

Country of Origin: USA.
Type: Two-seat light multi-purpose military helicopter.
Power Plant: One 650 shp (485 kW) Allison 250-C30R turboshaft.
Performance: (OH-58D) Max speed, 147 mph (237 km/h) at 4,000 ft (1 220 m); max cruise, 138 mph (222 km/h) at 2,000 ft (610 m); econ cruise, 127 mph (204 km/h) at 4,000 ft (1 220 m); max inclined climb, 1,540 ft/min (7,8 m/sec); hovering ceiling (in ground effect), 12,000+ ft (3 660+ m), (out of ground effect), 11,200 ft (3 415 m); range (max fuel), 345 mls (556 km).
Weights: Empty, 2,825 lb (1 281 kg); max take-off, 4,500 lb (2 041 kg).
Dimensions: Rotor diam, 35 ft 0 in (10,67 m); fuselage length, 33 ft 10 in (10,31 m).
Notes: The Model 406 AHIP (Army Helicopter Improvement Program) scout helicopter is a major upgrade of the US Army's OH-58A Kiowa, the first of five prototypes flying on 6 October 1983. Two hundred and forty-three OH-58As are being upgraded to armed OH-58D Kiowa Warrior configuration with mast-mounted sight and provision for four Hellfire air-to-surface or Stinger air-to-air missiles, two seven-round 2·75-in rocket pods or 7,62-mm or 12,7-mm gun pods. The Model 406 CS (Combat Scout) is a lighter and simplified variant of the OH-58D, which, first flown in June 1984, has been supplied to Saudi Arabia as the MH-58D, 15 being delivered in 1990. The Model 406 CS can carry two 20-mm cannon pods, four TOW 2 or Hellfire anti-armour missiles or Stinger air-to-air missiles.

BELL AH-1W SUPERCOBRA

Country of Origin: USA.

Type: Two-seat light anti-armour and attack helicopter.

Power Plant: Two 1,625 shp (1 213 kW) General Electric T700-401 turboshafts.

Performance: (At 14,750 lb/6 690 kg) Max speed, 196 mph (315 km/h) at sea level; max cruise, 173 mph (278 km/h); hovering ceiling (in ground effect), 14,750 ft (4 495 m), (out of ground effect), 3,000 ft (9,15 m); range (standard fuel), 365 mls (587 km) at sea level with standard fuel.

Weights: Empty, 10,200 lb (4 627 kg); max take-off, 14,750 lb (6 690 kg).

Dimensions: Rotor diam, 48 ft 0 in (14,63 m); fuselage length, 45 ft 6 in (13,87 m).

Notes: First flown on 16 November 1983, the AH-1W SuperCobra is an enhanced-capability derivative of the US Marine Corps' AH-1T SeaCobra, all surviving 39 examples of which being upgraded to -1W standard. Forty-four new-build AH-1Ws have been delivered to the USMC under a 1984 contract and deliveries to the service of a further 30 are scheduled to be completed by June 1991. The USMC Reserves have indicated a requirement for 42 AH-1W SuperCobras and five have been supplied to the Turkish Army. One AH-1W has been fitted with a four-blade bearingless rotor as the AH-1-4BW, and a larger four-bladed bearingless rotor is being developed for possible application to the USMC AH-1W fleet. The primary USMC AH-1W mission is the escort of troop-carrying helicopters.

BELL MODEL 214ST SUPERTRANSPORT

Country of Origin: USA.
Type: Commercial and military medium transport helicopter.
Power Plant: Two 1,625 shp (1,212 kW) General Electric CT7-2A turboshafts.
Performance: (At 17,500 lb/7 938 kg) Max cruise speed, 161 mph (259 km/h) at sea level, 159 mph (256 km/h) at 4,000 ft (1 220 m); max inclined climb, 1,780 ft/min (9,0 m/sec); hovering ceiling (in ground effect), 6,400 ft (1 950 m); range (max standard fuel), 533 mls (858 km) at 4,000 ft (1 220 m).
Weights: Max take-off, 17,500 lb (7 938 kg).
Dimensions: Rotor diam, 52 ft 0 in (15,85 m); fuselage length, 49 ft 3¾ in (15,02 m).
Notes: Developed originally for Iran and flown as a prototype for the first time in February 1977, the Model 214ST is a significantly improved derivative of the Model 214B BigLifter, customer deliveries having commenced early in 1982. The current production version has dual controls and standard seating for pilot, co-pilot and up to 18 passengers in three rows across the cabin plus a two-place bench seat on each side of the rotor mast. A non-retractable tubular skid-type or tricycle wheel-type undercarriage may be fitted, and a variety of special mission equipment has been developed and certified to suit the SuperTransport for service with the offshore oil industry. Military transport models have been delivered to Brunei (one), Iraq (45), Peru (11), Thailand (nine) and Venezuela (four). The Model 214ST is being replaced by the Model 230 (see page 230).

BELL MODEL 222UT

Country of Origin: USA.
Type: Six/eight-seat light utility and transport helicopter.
Power Plant: Two 684 shp (510 kW) Textron Lycoming LTS 101-750C-1 turboshafts.
Performance: Max speed, 179 mph (289 km/h) at 4,000 ft (1 220 m); econ cruise, 153 mph (246 km/h); hovering ceiling (in ground effect), 7,100 ft (2 165 m), (out of ground effect), 6,400 ft (1 950 m); max inclined climb, 1,680 ft/min (8,53 m/sec); range (max fuel and 20 min reserves), 380 mls (610 km).
Weights: Empty equipped, 4,874 lb (2 210 kg); max take-off, 8,250 lb (3 742 kg).
Dimensions: Rotor diam, 42 ft 0 in (12,80 m); fuselage length, 42 ft 2 in (12,85 m).
Notes: The first commercial light twin-engined helicopter to be built in the USA, the Model 222 was flown for the first time on 13 August 1976, the first customer delivery being effected on 16 January 1980. Progressive development led to the Model 222B which, with a larger main rotor and uprated engines, became the first transport category helicopter to be certificated by the FAA for single-pilot IFR flight without stability augmentation. The Model 222UT (Utility Twin) is similar to the 222B, apart from having a tubular skid rather than a retractable wheel undercarriage, and has standard seating for a pilot and six, seven or eight passengers. A corporate executive transport version of the basic helicopter, known as the Model 222B Executive, offers luxury accommodation for five or six passengers. A total of 182 examples of the Model 222 helicopter (all versions) has been built.

BELL MODEL 230

Country of Origin: USA (Canada).

Type: Six/ten-seat light utility and transport helicopter.

Power Plant: Two 700 shp (522 kW) Allison 250-C30G2 turboshafts.

Performance: Max cruise speed, 161 mph (259 km/h), (utility) 157 mph (252 km/h); range, 379 mls (609 km), (utility) 484 mls (780 km); endurance, 2·4 hrs, (utility) 3·0 hrs.

Weights: Empty (utility), 4,903 lb (2 224 kg); max take-off, 8,250 lb (3 742 kg).

Dimensions: Rotor diam, 42 ft 0 in (12,80 m); fuselage length, 42 ft 6¾ in (12,97 m).

Notes: The Model 230 is a derivative of the Model 222 which it will eventually replace, and is expected to fly in July 1991 and to be certificated in the following December with first customer deliveries expected in August 1992, eight Model 230s being completed in that year. To be manufactured by Bell Helicopter Textron's Canadian Division, the Model 230 will be available in both fixed-skid and retractable-wheel versions, and the first 50 will be Allison-engined, but subsequently the Textron Lycoming LTS 101 turboshaft will be offered as an option and it is likely that the two-bladed rotor will be replaced by a four-bladed rotor. It is also expected that, subsequent to the 15th production helicopter, Bell's liquid inertia vibration elimination system (LIVE) will be adopted. Among versions currently proposed is a medevac model with extra storage capacity for medical equipment, rupture-resistant fuel cells and self-sealing fuel fittings. Bell expects to produce 24–36 Model 230s annually.

BELL MODEL 412SP

Country of Origin: USA (Canada).
Type: Fifteen-seat utility transport helicopter.
Power Plant: One 1,400 shp (1,044 kW) Pratt & Whitney Canada PT6T-3B-1 Turbo Twin Pac twin turboshaft.
Performance: (At 11,900 lb/5 397 kg) Max speed, 161 mph (259 km/h) at sea level; max cruise, 143 mph (230 km/h); max inclined climb, 1,350 ft/min (6,86 m/sec); hovering ceiling (in ground effect), 1,400 ft (427 m), (out of ground effect at 10,500 lb/4 762 kg), 9,200 ft (2 805 m); max range (standard fuel), 408 mls (656 km) at sea level.
Weights: Empty (utility), 6,495 lb (2 946 kg); max take-off, 11,900 lb (5 397 kg).
Dimensions: Rotor diam, 46 ft 0 in (14,02 m); fuselage length, 42 ft 4¾ in (12,92 m).
Notes: Derived from the Model 212, the Model 412 entered flight test in August 1979, with customer deliveries commencing on 18 January 1981. Progressive development resulted in the Model 412SP, the suffix signifying Special Performance, this having an uprated transmission and an increased maximum take-off weight. Licence manufacture of the Model 412SP is undertaken in Indonesia by IPTN and in Italy by Agusta, all production by the parent company having been transferred from the USA to Canada at the beginning of 1989. Agusta has developed a multi-purpose military version named Griffon, customers for which have included the Italian Army, the Zimbabwe Air Force and the Ugandan Army. The parent company has also developed a military version of the Model 412SP.

BOEING HELICOPTERS MH-47E CHINOOK

Country of Origin: USA.
Type: Assault transport helicopter.
Power Plant: Two 4,110 shp (3,065 kW) Textron Lycoming T55-L-714 turboshafts with emergency rating of 5,028 shp (3,749 kW).
Performance: (CH-47D at 50,000 lb/22 679 kg) Max speed, 185 mph (298 km/h) at sea level; average cruise, 152 mph (245 km/h); max inclined climb, 1,522 ft/min (7,73 m/sec); hovering ceiling (out of ground effect), 5,000 ft (1 524 m).
Weights: (CH-47D) Empty, 23,149 lb (10 500 kg); loaded, 50,000 lb (22 679 kg); max take-off, 54,000 lb (24 494 kg).
Dimensions: Rotor diam (each), 60 ft 0 in (18,29 m); fuselage length (excluding refuelling probe), 51 ft 0 in (15,54 m).
Notes: The MH-47E, a prototype of which was rolled out on 6 December 1989, has been developed specifically for the US Army's Special Operations Forces and is intended to perform deep-penetration covert missions over a 345-mile (560-km) radius in adverse weather, day or night. The US Army requires 51 MH-47E Chinooks which are being converted from CH-47Cs with the first 17 being scheduled for delivery between January and September 1992. Possessing an essentially similar performance to that of the CH-47D (as above), the MH-47E possesses in-flight refuelling capability and is able to self-deploy to Europe. Accommodating up to 45 troops, the MH-47E has provision for installation of all-composite external fuel pods doubling the basic fuel capacity, has two window-mounted 0.5-in (12,7-mm) guns and is to be fitted with Stinger AAMs using FLIR (Forward-Looking Infra Red) for sighting.

DEUTSCHE AEROSPACE (MBB) BO 108

Country of Origin: Germany.
Type: Four/five-seat light technology demonstration helicopter.
Power Plant: Two 450 shp (335·5 kW) Allison 250-C20R-3, 509 shp (380 kW) Turboméca TM 319-1B or 531 shp (396 kW) Pratt & Whitney Canada PW205B turboshafts.
Performance: (Allison 250) Max cruise speed (approx), 168 mph (270 km/h) at 4,920 ft (1 500 m); econ cruise, 149 mph (240 km/h); max inclined climb, 1,810 ft/min (9·23 m/sec); hovering ceiling (in ground effect), 12,630–16,400 ft (3 850–5 000 m), (out of ground effect), 10,990 ft (3 350 m); max range, 497 mls (800 km).
Weights: Empty, 2,700 lb (1 225 kg); max take-off, 5,291 lb (2 400 kg).
Dimensions: Rotor diam, 32 ft 9¾ in (10,00 m); fuselage length, 31 ft 3 in (9,52 m).
Notes: The BO 108 was initiated as a technology demonstrator embodying new and advanced features, such as a completely hingeless main rotor, shallow transmission with special vibration absorbers, composite structures, etc. The first prototype was flown on 15 October 1988 with Allison 250 turboshafts, this being joined some two years later by a second prototype with cabin modifications and TM 319 engines. At the beginning of 1991, a decision had been taken to construct a third prototype with PW205B engines and to initiate series production with these engines. One aim of the BO 108 is to offer single-pilot IFR and a cost-effective stability augmentation system.

DEUTSCHE AEROSPACE (MBB)/KAWASAKI BK 117

Countries of Origin: Germany and Japan.

Type: Multi-purpose eight/twelve-seat helicopter.

Power Plant: Two 592 shp (442 kW) Textron Lycoming LTS 101-750B-1 turboshafts.

Performance: (BK 117B-1 at 7,055 lb/3 200 kg) Max speed, 172 mph (278 km/h) at sea level; max cruise, 154 mph (248 km/h); max inclined climb, 1,910 ft/min (9,7 m/sec); hovering ceiling (in ground effect), 9,600 ft (2 925 m), (out of ground effect), 7,500 ft (2 285 m); range (max standard fuel), 354 mls (570 km).

Weights: Basic empty, 3,807 lb (1 727 kg); max take-off, 7,055 lb (3 200 kg).

Dimensions: Rotor diam, 36 ft 1 in (11,00 m); fuselage length, 32 ft 6¼ in (9,91 m).

Notes: The BK 117 has been developed jointly by MBB of Germany, now the Helicopter and Military Aircraft Group of Deutsche Aerospace, and Kawasaki of Japan. It is manufactured by the single-source method, each company producing the components that it has developed, these also being supplied to assembly lines in Canada (MBB Helicopters Canada) and Indonesia (IPTN). The BK 117B-1 is currently the standard production version, having been introduced at the beginning of 1989. Customer deliveries of the initial BK 117A-1 began early in 1981, the progressively improved A-3 and A-4 finally giving place to the B-1. Some 270 BK 117 helicopters had been delivered worldwide by the beginning of 1991.

EH INDUSTRIES EH 101 (MERLIN)

Countries of Origin: United Kingdom and Italy.

Type: Military and commercial transport, utility and shipboard anti-submarine warfare helicopter.

Power Plant: Three 1,920 shp (1,432 kW) General Electric CT7-6 or (naval version) 1,714 shp (1,278 kW) T700-GE-401A turboshafts.

Performance: (CT7-6 engines) Typical cruise speed, 173 mph (278 km/h); best endurance speed, 104 mph (167 km/h); range (standard fuel with reserves and 30 passengers), 580 mls (925 km); ferry range (commercial version with standard fuel and reserves), 1,093 mls (1 760 km).

Weights: Empty operational (naval), 20,500 lb (9 275 kg), (military), 19,840 lb (9 000 kg), (commercial), 19,695 lb (8 993 kg); max take-off (naval), 29,830 lb (13 530 kg), (military and commercial), 31,500 lb (14 288 kg).

Dimensions: Rotor diam, 61 ft 0 in (18,59 m); fuselage length, 64 ft 0 in (19,51 m).

Notes: Developed by EH Industries in which Westland Helicopters of the UK and Agusta of Italy participate, the EH 101 is to be of single-source manufacture with assembly lines in both the UK and Italy. The first of nine pre-production helicopters was flown on 9 October 1987, the fifth and sixth being dedicated to development of the naval ASW model (which is to be known as the Merlin in Royal Navy service), the seventh represents the military rear ramp variant, and the eighth and ninth (flown on 16 January 1991) represent the commercial Heliliner version. Production is expected to commence in 1992.

235

EUROCOPTER TIGER

Countries of Origin: France and Germany.

Type: Tandem two-seat anti-armour and ground support helicopter.

Power Plant: Two 1,285 shp (958 kW) MTU/Rolls-Royce/Turboméca MTR 390 turboshafts.

Performance: (Estimated at 11,905 lb/5 400 kg) Max cruise speed, 174 mph (280 km/h); normal cruise, 155 mph (250 km/h); max inclined climb, 1,970+ ft/min (10+ m/sec); hovering ceiling (out of ground effect), 6,560+ ft (2 000+ m); endurance (including 20 min reserves), 2·85 hrs.

Weights: Basic empty, 7,275 lb (3 300 kg); mission take-off, 11,685–12,346 lb (5 300–5 600 kg); max overload, 13,227 lb (6 000 kg).

Dimensions: Rotor diam, 42 ft 7¾ in (13,00 m); fuselage length, 45 ft 11¼ in (14,00 m).

Notes: Rolled out on 4 February 1991 and scheduled to enter flight test in April, with a second prototype flying in 1992, three more Tiger prototypes will appear at six-monthly intervals. The Tiger is being developed by Eurocopter GmbH, work being shared between Aérospatiale of France and the Helicopter Division (MBB) of Deutsche Aerospace of Germany. The Tiger is projected in three versions, the HAC and HAP for the French Army (*Hélicoptère d'Appui Protection* and *Hélicoptère Anti-Char*) for escort and fire support and for anti-tank tasks respectively, and the PAH-2 (*Panzerabwehr-Hubschrauber*) anti-tank helicopter for the German Army. Estimated requirements are 75 HAPs and 140 HACs for France and 212 PAH-2s for Germany.

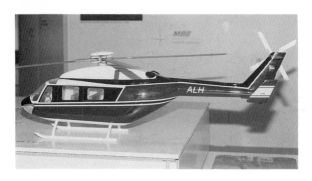

HAL ALH

Country of Origin: India.

Type: Multi-role civil and military light helicopter.

Power Plant: Two 1,000 shp (746 kW) Turboméca TM 333-2B turboshafts.

Performance: (Estimated) Max speed, 180 mph (290 km/h) at sea level; hovering ceiling (out of ground effect), 9,850+ ft (3 000+ m); range (with 1,543-lb/700-kg payload), 248 mls (400 km) at sea level.

Weights: Empty (Army/Air Force version), 4,885 lb /2 216 kg), (Navy version), 5,185 lb (2 352 kg); max take-off (Army/Air Force), 8,818 lb (4 000 kg), (Navy), 11,023 lb (5 000 kg).

Dimensions: (Approximate) Rotor diam, 43 ft 7 in (13,20 m); length overall (both rotors turning), 52 ft 0¾ in (15,87 m).

Notes: The ALH (Advanced Light Helicopter) has been developed by Hindustan Aeronautics Limited (HAL) with the assistance of the Helicopter and Military Aircraft Group (MBB) of Deutsche Aerospace, and the first of four prototypes is expected to enter flight test mid 1991 with series production commencing 1993–94. Versions are proposed for the three armed services, that for the Army performing air assault, re-supply of heliborne forces, aerial minelaying and anti-tank missions, the Navy version fulfilling CASEVAC, communications, SAR and ASW roles, and the Air Force variant performing air crew rescue, off-shore operations, logistical support and light transportation missions as well as CASEVAC. Carrying two crew members and up to 10 passengers, the ALH has four-bladed hingeless main and tail rotors.

KAMOV KA-29TB (HELIX-B)

Country of Origin: USSR.

Type: Combat transport helicopter.

Power Plant: Two 2,225 shp (1,660 kW) Leningrad Klimov (Isotov) TV3-117V turboshafts.

Performance: Max speed, 165 mph (265 km/h) at sea level; max cruise, 143 mph (230 km/h); max inclined climb, 2,380 ft/min (12,09 m/sec); max range, 310 mls (500 km).

Weights: Max take-off, 26,455 lb (12 000 kg).

Dimensions: Rotor diam (each), 53 ft 9½ in (16,40 m); fuselage length (excluding nose probe), 37 ft 8¾ in (11,50 m).

Notes: The Ka-29TB (*transportno-boyevoya,* or combat transport) is a development of the Ka-27 ASW (Helix-A) and SAR (Helix-D) helicopter, an export version of which is designated Ka-28. First seen in 1989, the Ka-29TB is primarily a transport for seaborne assault troops and for the support of amphibious landings by the delivery of precision-guided weapons. Possessing a wider flight deck than that of the Ka-27, a shallow, curved nose and stub wings for carrying ordnance, the Ka-29TB is heavily armoured, has a four-barrel rotary 7,62-mm gun behind a downward-articulated door in the starboard side of the nose and sensor pods beneath the nose. Four pylons can carry AT-6 Spiral radio-guided tube-launched missiles or 57-mm or 80-mm rocket packs. The Ka-29TB can accommodate 14–18 combat-equipped troops on sidewall seats. The Ka-27 Helix-A and Ka-27PS Helix-D (see 1989/90 edition) serve aboard the carriers *Kuznyetsov* and *Varyag* (formerly *Tbilisi* and *Riga*), and the *Kiev*-class *Gorshkov* and *Novorossiysk* carrier/cruisers.

KAMOV KA-32 (HELIX-C)

Country of Origin: USSR.

Type: Civil utility helicopter.

Power Plant: Two 2,225 shp (1,660 kW) Leningrad Klimov (Isotov) TV3-117V turboshafts.

Performance: (At 24,250 lb/11 000 kg) Max speed, 155 mph (250 km/h) at sea level; max cruise, 143 mph (230 km/h); hovering ceiling (out of ground effect), 11,480 ft (3 500 m); service ceiling, 19,685 ft (6 000 m); range (with max fuel), 497 mls (800 km); endurance, 4·5 hrs.

Weights: Normal loaded, 24,250 lb (11 000 kg); max flight weight with slung load, 27,775 lb (12 600 kg).

Dimensions: Rotor diam (each), 52 ft 2 in (15,90 m); fuselage length, 37 ft 1 in (11,30 m).

Notes: A civil derivative of the Ka-27 ASW and SAR helicopter, the Ka-32 appeared in prototype form in 1981, and two versions have been produced, the Ka-32S for deployment aboard icebreakers and the Ka-32T basic transport and flying crane. The latter has more limited avionics and its tasks include the transportation of internal and external freight, and of up to 16 passengers on sidewall and rear bulkhead folding seats. The Ka-32S is equipped for operation in adverse weather conditions and over terrain devoid of landmarks. Its tasks include ice patrol, the guidance of ships through icefields, support of offshore drilling rigs, maritime search and rescue, and the loading and unloading of ships. Flight can be maintained on one engine and the Ka-32 possesses an automatic control system. Thirty plus Ka-32s are in service with Aeroflot.

KAMOV KA-136 (HOKUM)

Country of Origin: USSR.

Type: Two-seat combat helicopter.

Power Plant: Two 2,200 shp (1,640 kW) Leningrad Klimov (Isotov) TV3-117 turboshafts.

Performance: (Estimated) Max speed, 220 mph (354 km/h); max continuous cruise, 200 mph (322 km/h); combat radius, 155 mls (250 km).

Weights: (Estimated) Max take-off, 16,500 lb (7 500 kg).

Dimensions: (Estimated) Rotor diam (each), 45 ft 10 in (14,00 m); overall length, 44 ft 3 in (13,50 m).

Notes: Assigned the NATO reporting name Hokum and believed to possess the design bureau designation of Ka-136, the two-seat Kamov combat helicopter illustrated above first became known in the summer of 1984, and only prototypes were believed to have flown by the beginning of 1991, although the US Department of Defense anticipated that it would enter service in the early 'nineties. Retaining the coaxial, contra-rotating rotor arrangement that has characterised earlier helicopters from the Kamov bureau, the Hokum is believed to possess a primary armament of air-to-air missiles, packs of unguided rockets and a rapid-fire gun, indicating that its principal task is that of helicopter interception, presumably by day and night, and in adverse weather. Other roles are likely to include close air support and escort of Ka-29TB helicopters in amphibious assault operations. Unlike other combat helicopters, the two crew members of Hokum appear to be seated side by side in a heavily armoured cockpit.

McDONNELL DOUGLAS AH-64A APACHE

Country of Origin: USA.
Type: Tandem two-seat attack helicopter.
Power Plant: Two 1,696 shp (1,265 kW) General Electric T700-GE-701 turboshafts.
Performance: (At 14,445 lb/6 552 kg) Max speed, 184 mph (296 km/h); typical mission cruise (at 15,780 lb/7 158 kg), 169 mph (272 km/h); max inclined climb, 2,500 ft/min (12,7 m/sec); hovering ceiling (in ground effect), 15,000 ft (4 570 m), (out of ground effect), 11,500 ft (3 505 m); max range (internal fuel), 300 mls (482 km).
Weights: Empty, 10,760 lb (4 881 kg); max take-off, 21,000 lb (9 525 kg).
Dimensions: Rotor diam, 48 ft 0 in (14,63 m); fuselage length, 48 ft 1⅞ in (14,70 m).
Notes: First of two YAH-64 prototypes of the Apache was flown on 30 September 1975, and deliveries to the US Army commenced in 1984, with some 630 delivered by the beginning of 1991 when production was continuing at six Apaches monthly with the final US Army helicopter scheduled to be delivered in September 1993. All AH-64As are to be retrofitted with the 1,857 shp (1,385 kW) T700-GE-701C turboshaft and 227 are to be upgraded to so-called Longbow configuration. This embraces the installation of Longbow millimetre-wave radar and provision for the RF seeker-equipped Hellfire missiles. The current AH-64A has a single-barrel 30-mm gun and may carry up to 16 laser-guided Hellfire missiles. Nineteen have been supplied to Israel and 24 to Egypt.

McDONNELL DOUGLAS MD 520N

Country of Origin: USA.

Type: Five/seven-seat utility helicopter.

Power Plant: One 375 hp (280 kW) Allison 250-C20R-2 turboshaft.

Performance: Max cruise speed, 156 mph (251 km/h) at sea level; max inclined climb, 1,820 ft/min (9,25 m/sec); hovering ceiling (in ground effect), 10,100 ft (3 080 m), (out of ground effect), 7,310 ft (2 230 m); service ceiling, 15,800 ft (4 815 m); max range (standard fuel), 285 mls (458 km) at 5,000 ft (1 525 m).

Weights: Empty, 1,534 lb (696 kg); max take-off (normal), 3,350 lb (1 519 kg), (with external load), 3,850 lb (1 746 kg).

Dimensions: Rotor diam, 28 ft 3½ in (8,62 m); fuselage length, 25 ft 0 in (7,62 m).

Notes: The MD 520N (described above) and the MD 530N (illustrated above) are the first production NOTAR (NO TAil Rotor) helicopters and differ essentially in power, the latter having an Allison 250-C30 turboshaft rated at 650 shp (485 kW). Evolved respectively from the orthodox tail rotor MD 500 and MD 530, a prototype of the MD 530N flying on 29 December 1989 and of the 520N in January 1990, these helicopters entered production in 1990, with customer deliveries having been scheduled to commence early 1991 when production tempo was building up to 7·5 helicopters monthly. By comparison with the tail rotor MD 500 and 530 (see 1989/90 edition), the NOTAR derivatives have an increased-diameter rotor, new tail-boom, NOTAR fan and new tail surfaces.

MIL MI-26 (HALO)

Country of Origin: USSR.

Type: Military and civil heavy-lift helicopter.

Power Plant: Two 11,240 shp (8,380 kW) ZMKB Progress (Lotarev) D-136 turboshafts.

Performance: Max speed, 183 mph (295 km/h); normal cruise, 158 mph (255 km/h); hovering ceiling (in ground effect), 14,765 ft (4 500 m), (out of ground effect), 5,905 ft (1 800 m); range (at 109,127 lb/49 500 kg), 310 mls (500 km), (at 123,457 lb/ 56 000 kg), 497 mls (800 km).

Weights: Empty, 62,169 lb (28 200 kg); normal loaded, 109,227 lb (49 500 kg); max take-off, 123,457 lb (56 000 kg).

Dimensions: Rotor diam, 104 ft 11⅞ in (32,00 m); fuselage length, 110 ft 7¾ in (33,73 m).

Notes: Flown for the first time on 14 December 1977, the Mi-26 is the heaviest and most powerful helicopter yet to achieve production status, and the first to operate successfully with an eight-bladed main rotor. At the beginning of 1991, an uprated version of the Mi-26 with rotor blades entirely of composites and a 48,500-lb (22 000-kg) maximum payload was under development. The current model has a crew of five and a four-seat passenger compartment aft of the flight deck, possible loads include some 85 combat-equipped troops, 40 casualty stretchers plus medical attendants, two airborne infantry combat vehicles or a 44,090-lb (20 000-kg) container. The Mi-26 attained operational capability with the SovAF in 1985, some 60 reportedly being in service, and deliveries to the Indian Air Force began in 1986.

MIL MI-28 (HAVOC)

Country of Origin: USSR.

Type: Tandem two-seat anti-armour and attack helicopter.

Power Plant: Two 2,200 shp (1,640 kW) Leningrad Klimov (Isotov) TV3-117 turboshafts.

Performance: Max speed (design), 227 mph (365 km/h); max cruise, 177 mph (285 km/h); hovering ceiling (out of ground effect), 11,800 ft (3 600 m); service ceiling, 18,865 ft (5 750 m); mission range, 286–298 mls (460–480 km) at 177 mph (285 km/h).

Weights: Basic empty, 14,330 lb (6 500 kg); normal loaded, 22,928 lb (10 400 kg); max take-off, 25,133 lb (11 400 kg).

Dimensions: Rotor diam, 56 ft 5 in (17,20 m); fuselage length, 55 ft 3$\frac{1}{2}$ in (16,85 m).

Notes: The first of three prototypes of the Mi-28 was flown on 10 November 1982, subsequent development being rather protracted, with initial operational capability being expected in 1992. Currently the most powerful of dedicated combat helicopters, the Mi-28 features titanium and composite armour to protect the crew members, fuel tanks and vital items of equipment. Armament includes a 30-mm turret-mounted cannon under the fuselage nose and two pylons under each wing can each take up to 1,058 lb (480 kg) of ordnance, a typical load comprising 16 beam-riding AT-6 Spiral tube-launched anti-armour missiles and two pods each containing 20 rockets of 57-mm or 80-mm calibre. Versions of the Mi-28 are being developed for naval amphibious assault support, night attack and air-to-air missions. The Mi-28 superficially resembles the AH-64 Apache.

MIL MI-35P (HIND-F)

Country of Origin: USSR.

Type: Assault and anti-armour helicopter.

Power Plant: Two 2,200 shp (1,640 kW) Leningrad Klimov (Isotov) TV3-117 turboshafts.

Performance: Max speed, 208 mph (335 km/h); max continuous cruise, 168 mph (270 km/h); hovering ceiling (out of ground effect), 4,921 ft (1 500 m); range (with five per cent fuel reserve), 280 mls (450 km); endurance, 4·0 hrs.

Weights: Empty equipped, 18,078 lb (8 200 kg); normal loading, 24,692 lb (11 200 kg); max take-off, 26,455 lb (12 000 kg).

Dimensions: Rotor diam, 56 ft 9 in (17,30 m); fuselage length, 57 ft 5 in (17,51 m).

Notes: The Mi-35P is the current export version of the Mi-24P Hind-F and supplants the Mi-25 which was the export version of the Mi-24D Hind-D. Both the Mi-24P and Mi-35P have a fixed twin-barrel 30-mm cannon (the 'P' suffix in the designations signifying *pushka*, or cannon) on the starboard side of the fuselage replacing the undernose turreted 12,7-mm multi-barrel rotary machine gun of the Mi-24D and Mi-25. The export version of the Mi-24W Hind-E is designated Mi-35, this having modified wingtip launchers and four underwing pylons to take up to 12 beam-riding AT-6 Spiral tube-launched missiles. The Mi-35P provides tandem seating for a pilot (at the rear) and weapons operator, a flight mechanic between the pilot's cockpit and the main cabin, and an eight-man assault squad. Up to 3,300 lb (1 500 kg) of external ordnance may be carried and total Mi-24/25/35 production exceeds 2,300 helicopters.

PZL SWIDNIK W-3 SOKOL

Country of Origin: Poland.
Type: Medium transport and multi-role helicopter.
Power Plant: Two 880 shp (662 kW) PZL-10W (Omsk/Glushenkov TVD-10B) turboshafts with emergency rating of 1,134 shp (845·5 kW) for 2·5 min.
Performance: Max speed, 158 mph (255 km/h); max cruise, 146 mph (235 km/h); econ cruise, 137 mph (220 km/h); max inclined climb, 1,673 ft/min (8·5 m/sec); hovering ceiling (in ground effect), 9,845 ft (3 000 m), (out of ground effect), 6,890 ft (2 100 m); range (standard fuel and 5% reserves), 422 mls (680 km).
Weights: Basic operational empty, 8,002 lb (3 630 kg); normal take-off, 13,448 lb (6 100 kg); max take-off, 14,110 lb (6 400 kg).
Dimensions: Rotor diam, 51 ft 6 in (15,70 m); fuselage length, 46 ft 7½ in (14,21 m).
Notes: The Sokól (Falcon) has been the subject of protracted development, the first of five prototypes having flown on 16 November 1979 and full certification not being obtained until 10 April 1990. Six pre-series aircraft had been built by 1990 when series production was initiated, a Soviet order of 35 helicopters of this type being announced. The Sokól has a flight crew of two and can accommodate up to 12 passengers, an ambulance version carrying four casualty stretchers and a medical attendant. A maximum of 4,630 lb (2 100 kg) of cargo can be carried internally, the same weight being carried as a slung load. A SAR variant is under development. Between 20 and 30 W-3s have been ordered by the Burmese Air Force.

ROBINSON R44

Country of Origin: USA.

Type: Four-seat light utility helicopter.

Power Plant: One 260 hp (194 kW) Textron Lycoming O-540 six-cylinder horizontally-opposed engine derated to 225 hp (168 kW).

Performance: Max speed, 142 mph (228 km/h); cruise speed (at 75% power), 130 mph (209 km/h) at sea level; econ cruise, 96 mph (154 mph); max inclined climb, 1,250 ft/min (6,35 m/sec); hovering ceiling (in ground effect), 6,800 ft (2 073 m); max operating ceiling, 14,000 ft (4 267 m).

Weights: Empty weight, 1,350 lb (612 kg); max take-off, 2,350 lb (1 066 kg).

Dimensions: Rotor diam, 33 ft 0 in (10,06 m).

Notes: Incorporating many of the features of the current production side-by-side two-seat R22, the R44 was flown for the first time on 31 March 1990, and is expected to retail at approximately half the price of an equivalent turbine-powered helicopter. Certification of the R44 is targeted for 1992, with first customer deliveries commencing shortly thereafter. The R22, of which some 1,675 had been delivered by the beginning of 1991, with 400 of these being produced during 1990, is of fundamentally similar design to the R44, both placing emphasis on simplicity and featuring low-corrosion two-blade semi-articulated rotors and normally aspirated engines. The standard version of the R22 is the Beta (see 1989/90 edition) which, with floats, is known as the Mariner. The R22 has been widely adopted as a tuitional helicopter.

SIKORSKY S-80M (MH-53E SEA DRAGON)

Country of Origin: USA.

Type: Mine countermeasures helicopter.

Power Plant: Three 4,380 shp (3,266 kW) General Electric T64-GE-416 turboshafts.

Performance: (At 56,000 lb/25 400 kg) Max speed, 196 mph (315 km/h) at sea level; max continuous cruise, 173 mph (278 km/h); max inclined climb (with 25,000 lb/11 340 kg payload), 2,500 ft/min (12,7 m/sec); hovering ceiling (in ground effect), 11,550 ft (3 520 m), (out of ground effect), 9,500 ft (2 895 m); service ceiling, 18,500 ft (5 640 m).

Weights: Empty, 36,336 lb (16,482 kg); max take-off, 69,750 lb (31 640 kg).

Dimensions: Rotor diam, 79 ft 0 in (24,08 m); fuselage length, 73 ft 4 in (22,35 m).

Notes: The S-80 is an export version of the CH-53E Super Stallion heavy duty helicopter of the US Navy and Marine Corps, the S-80M (illustrated and described above) being the export form of the MH-53E Sea Dragon. The Japanese Maritime Self-Defence Force is procuring 12 examples of the S-80M, the first of these having been handed over on 30 November 1989. The S-80M, like the MH-53E, is able to tow mechanical, acoustic and magnetic hydrofoil mine sweeping gear through the water. The first pre-production MH-53E flew for the first time on 1 September 1983, and deliveries to the US Navy began on 26 June 1986. By comparison with the S-80E and CH-53E, the S-80M and MH-53E have greatly enlarged sponsons which carry nearly one thousand US gal (833 Imp gal) of fuel.

SIKORSKY S-70A (DESERT HAWK)

Country of Origin: USA.

Type: Tactical utility transport helicopter.

Power Plant: Two 1,857 shp (1 385 kW) General Electric T700-GE-701C turboshafts.

Performance: (At 16,994 lb/7 708 kg) Max speed, 184 mph (296 km/h) at sea level; max cruise, 167 mph (268 km/h) at 4,000 ft (1 220 m); hovering ceiling (in ground effect), 9,500 ft (2 895 m), (out of ground effect), 5,600 ft (1 705 m); range (max internal fuel and 30 min reserves), 373 mls (600 km), (with two 230 US gal/870 l pylon tanks), 1,012 mls (1 630 km).

Weights: Empty, 11,284 lb (5 118 kg); max take-off, 22,000 lb (9 979 kg).

Dimensions: Rotor diam, 53 ft 8 in (16,23 m); fuselage length, 50 ft 0¾ in (15,26 m).

Notes: The S-70A is the export tactical utility version of the UH-60A Black Hawk assault transport of the US Army and has been supplied in Desert Hawk configuration (above) to Saudi Arabia. The Desert Hawk has 15 troop seats, special radio equipment and a blade erosion protection system. Two essentially similar helicopters (S-70A-5s) have been supplied to the Philippines and 39 (S-70A-9s) to the Royal Australian Air Force. Variants of the UH-60A supplied to the US Army include the EH-60C electronic countermeasures helicopter, and the MH-60A and MH-60K special operations helicopters. The VH-60A is a US Marine Corps-operated VIP transport version and the MH-60G Pave Hawk is a USAF rescue variant. Westland has a licence to build the WH-60L in the UK as the WS 70L.

SIKORSKY S-70B (SH-60)

Country of Origin: USA.

Type: (SH-60) Anti-submarine warfare and anti-ship surveillance and targeting helicopter and (HH-60) strike-rescue and special warfare support helicopter.

Power Plant: Two 1,900 shp (1 417 kW) General Electric T700-GE-401C turboshafts.

Performance: (SH-60B at 20,244 lb/9 183 kg) Max speed, 167 mph (269 km/h); max cruise, 155 mph (249 km/h) at 5,000 ft (1 525 km); time on station (at radius of 57 mls/92 km), 3·86 hrs.

Weights: Empty (ASW mission), 13,648 lb (6 191 kg); mission weight, 20,244 lb (9 182 kg); max take-off (utility), 21,884 lb (9 926 kg).

Dimensions: Rotor diam, 53 ft 8 in (16,36 m); fuselage length, 50 ft 0¾ in (15,26 m).

Notes: The S-70B has been delivered to the US Navy in two ASW versions, the SH-60B Seahawk and the SH-60F Ocean Hawk (illustrated above), and for strike-rescue and the support of special forces as the HH-60H. The SH-60B was the designation assigned to the S-70B after this helicopter was selected as the winning LAMPS (Light Airborne Multi-Purpose System) Mk III, the first of five prototypes flying on 11 February 1983, the first production helicopter following on 12 December 1979. Whereas the SH-60B operates from frigates and destroyers, the SH-60F has the LAMPS Mk III avionics removed and operates from carriers in protection of a carrier battle group. The SH-60B is being supplied to Japan's Maritime Self-Defence Force.

SIKORSKY S-76

Country of Origin: USA.
Type: Light general purpose and transport helicopter.
Power Plant: Two 681 shp (508 kW) Turboméca Arriel 1S or 960 shp (716 kW) Pratt & Whitney Canada PT6B-36 turboshafts.
Performance: (PT6B engines at 11,700 lb/5 307 kg) Max speed, 178 mph (287 km/h) at sea level; max cruise, 167 mph (269 km/h); econ cruise, 151 mph (243 km/h); max inclined climb, 1,500 ft/min (7,62 m/sec); hovering ceiling (in ground effect), 8,200 ft (2 500 m), (out of ground effect), 5,400 ft (1 646 km); range (standard fuel and 30 min reserves), 359 mls (578 km) at 150 mph (241 km/h) at 3,000 ft (915 m).
Weights: Empty, 6,656 lb (3 019 kg); max take-off, 11,700 lb (5 307 kg).
Dimensions: Rotor diam, 44 ft 0 in (13,41 m); fuselage length, 43 ft 4½ in (13,22 m).
Notes: The S-76 12-passenger commercial helicopter was flown on 13 March 1977, customer deliveries commencing early in 1979. The S-76 Mk II, introduced in March 1982, embodied numerous refinements and its Allison 250-C30 turboshafts had a five per cent higher take-off rating at 650 shp (522 kW). The S-76B, which first flew on 22 June 1984, differed primarily in having PT6B-36 turboshafts (see above), and the S-76A offered Arriel turboshafts as an option, first flying with these in 1987. Since then the Turboméca power plant has been available as a retrofit. The S-76C has the basic airframe and drivetrain of the S-76B mated with Arriel turboshafts, and the H-76 Eagle is a military development of the S-76B.

WESTLAND SUPER LYNX

Country of Origin: United Kingdom.
Type: Multi-role maritime helicopter.
Power Plant: Two 1,120 shp (835 kW) Rolls-Royce Gem 42-1 turboshafts.
Performance: Max continuous cruise speed, 159 mph (256 km/h); max endurance speed, 81 mph (130 km/h); max inclined climb, 1,970 ft/min (10 m/sec); range (anti-surface vessel mission with four anti-ship missiles and 20 min reserves), 265 mls (426 km), (search and rescue), 391 mls (630 km).
Weights: Operational empty (search and rescue), 8,064 lb (3 658 kg); max take-off, 11,300 lb (5 125 kg).
Dimensions: Rotor diam, 42 ft 0 in (12,80 m); length (rotors folded), 43 ft 5$\frac{1}{4}$ in (13,24 m).
Notes: An upgraded export version of the basic Westland helicopter and approximating to the Royal Navy's Lynx HAS Mk 8, the Super Lynx has been supplied to South Korea as the Lynx Mk 99, the first of 12 having flown on 16 November 1989. The South Korean Super Lynx has Seaspray Mk 3 360-deg scan radar in a chin fairing and can carry four Sea Skua or two Penguin anti-ship missiles. It is to be deployed aboard *Gearing* and *Sumner* class destroyers. Five Super Lynx are also being procured by Portugal (two being converted from ex-Royal Navy Lynx HAS Mk 3s) for deployment from the *Vasco da Gama* class frigates. An equivalent upgrading of the land-based Lynx is known as the Battlefield Lynx, the British Army Air Corps version being the Lynx AH Mk 9. More than 370 Lynx (all versions) had been sold by the beginning of 1991.

INDEX OF AIRCRAFT TYPES